All-Star or All Alone?

"It was really nice of you to mention your teammates on television last night!" Terry exclaimed, turning around. "We really appreciate it. I mean, you can't thank us in public because you did it all on your own, right?"

That was it for Breezy. The last straw. Her own teammates — her friends — thought she was an egomaniac. She would have expected it from Lindsay and her clones, but not from her own friends. That really hurt.

"Last time I checked," Breezy began, wanting to hurt them back, "no one else on the team pitched a no-hitter. Can I help it if I've got more talent than anyone else?"

Breezy didn't wait for an answer, but spun on her heel and walked down the hall toward her locker. She had to get away. She was really angry — and she definitely didn't want them to see how upset and hurt she was, too.

THE PINK PARROTS

NO-HITTER

Created by Lucy Ellis

By Leah Jerome

A *SPORTS ILLUSTRATED FOR KIDS* BOOK

First Edition

Library of Congress Cataloging-in-Publication Data
Jerome, Leah
   No hitter / by Leah Jerome ; created by Lucy Ellis ; [interior line-art by Jane Davila].
     p. cm.—(The Pink parrots ; #6)
   "A Sports illustrated for kids book."
   Summary: Breezy's achievement in pitching the first no-hitter in league history causes problems when she doesn't give her team any credit for her success.
   ISBN 0-316-47427-4
   [1. Sports — Fiction. 2. Baseball—Fiction. 3. Interpersonal relations—Fiction.]
I. Title. II. Series.
PZ7.J55214No1990
[Fic]—dc20   91-14761

10 9 8 7 6 5 4 3 2 1

SEM

For further information regarding this title, write to Little, Brown and Company, 34 Beacon Street, Boston, MA 02108

Published simultaneously in Canada by Little, Brown & Company (Canada) Limited

Printed in the United States of America

Created by Lucy Ellis
Written by Leah Jerome
Cover art by Gary Glover
Interior line art by Jane Davila
Produced By Angel Entertainment, Inc.

1

"One more," Breezy Hawk mumbled under her breath as she walked off the pitcher's mound at the end of the fifth inning. "I only have to make it through one more inning."

Breezy walked over to the dugout and sat down on the bench without looking at any of her teammates. She took off her pink baseball cap and tightened her dark blonde ponytail. Breezy was the captain of the Pink Parrots, the only all-girls baseball team in the Eastern Maryland Baseball League (Emblem). The Parrots were playing Tony's Pizzeria and were up 2-0.

Breezy's best friend, Kim Yardley, who played shortstop for the Parrots, came running into the dugout. Stopping short when she saw Breezy, Kim slowly walked over to her friend and sat down. She put her hand on Breezy's shoulder, but didn't say anything.

"I can't believe it, Breezy!" Betsy Winston, the centerfielder, exclaimed. "A no-hitter! This is unreal!"

Breezy had pitched five innings without giving up a

hit. No one had ever pitched a no-hitter in Emblem before. Ever.

"Well, she hasn't done it yet," Andrea Campbell added. The third baseman looked at Breezy and blew a big bubble with her gum. "And you know what they say? It ain't over until it's over."

"Guys!" Kim yelled, as Breezy jumped up and started pacing back and forth in the dugout. "Shut up!"

"What?" Betsy asked, sounding a little confused. "What did we do?"

Breezy shook her head in disgust. Sometimes she forgot that most of her teammates did not live and breathe baseball as she did. She and Kim had started this team at the beginning of the season because they were tired of the pine-time Coach Carpenter kept giving them on the Mitchell Lumber team bench. Only Breezy, Kim, and Terry DiSunno, the catcher, had really known anything about the game. While it was true that most of the girls on the team had learned a lot since then, they still didn't know some of the traditions. Like you never, ever, ever talk about a no-hitter in progress. Never.

"What?" Betsy asked again.

"You might jinx Breezy," Terry practically growled. "Don't talk about it. Don't even *think* about it until the game's over. Okay?"

"But it's not like Breezy gets this kind of chance every day," Betsy protested. "I mean, she usually doesn't pitch more than three innings a game."

Breezy knew that was definitely true. Emblem pitchers could pitch only six innings a week. Since each team had two games a week, coaches split their pitchers every game. It was almost unheard of for a single pitcher to pitch the entire six innings in a game, because he or she would be lost for the next game.

But Breezy had been on the disabled list for almost a month after a major collision at home plate, and this was her first game back. And because the Parrots didn't have another game until the following week, there was nothing to stop Breezy from pitching the whole game.

"It's very bad luck to talk about it!" Kim exclaimed. "Right, Ro?"

Rose Ann DiMona, the Pink Parrots coach and sponsor, nodded. "That's right," she agreed. "Besides, if Breezy doesn't want us to mention it, then we should respect her wishes and keep mum. Okay?"

Looking at all the girls on her team, Ro waited until everyone nodded. Breezy glanced thankfully at their coach, glad that she had put a stop to the chatter. Breezy had had her reservations about Ro when Ro had first volunteered to sponsor and coach the team. Ro was the owner of the Pink Parrot Beauty Salon and Breezy never would have picked a *beauty salon* as a sponsor, or a hair stylist as a coach. But Breezy had known that she couldn't even get her team registered in Emblem until she had a sponsor. And, as it turned out, Ro had more than proved herself to be an excellent coach.

Of course, Breezy still thought Ro dressed sort of weird. Today, the coach was wearing a hot pink lycra wrestler's unitard over her Parrots jersey. Her hot pink high-top sneakers only added to the outfit, Breezy figured. Ro wore something pink practically every day and Breezy really hated the color pink.

Ro was definitely not like the other coaches in Emblem. But as long as she kept the Parrots winning, that was all that mattered. And Ro knew baseball inside and out. Growing up, she had been a definite baseball brat — her father had played in the major leagues briefly and her brother was now on a Baltimore Orioles farm team. What Ro didn't know about baseball wasn't worth knowing.

Ro pulled out her zebra-striped clipboard and snapped her gum. "Okay, birds," she continued. "Here's the lineup. Andrea, Betsy, Breezy. Let's not get overconfident here. It only takes an inning for them to take back the game. Stay focused."

Breezy started looking for her favorite bat. It was one of the few wooden ones left in the league — everyone was totally into aluminum now. She was really glad that she was batting this inning. It took her mind off her . . . her pitching.

Looking out at the field, Breezy noticed that D.J. Hinds, Tony's Pizzeria's relief pitcher, was struggling with his warm-up pitches. Pat Julius, Tony's star pitcher, had not allowed a run for the first three innings. Then

D.J. had come in in the fourth and given up two runs. Maybe the Parrots could get a few runs now and get a good cushion. Breezy usually liked the challenge of coming from behind, but somehow, in this case, she thought she might have an easier time if she wasn't worried about the outcome of the game and could concentrate on her pitching.

Breezy slipped a weighted ring, called a donut, on her wooden bat and started swinging it over her head to loosen up her shoulders. She watched as Andrea stepped up to the plate.

"Come on, Andrea!" Breezy shouted. "Let's get something going!"

Andrea dug her right cleat into the dirt in the batter's box and faced the pitcher. D.J. adjusted his cap and then went into his windup. His first pitch was so far inside, Andrea had to jump back to avoid getting hit.

"A walk's as good as a hit!" Breezy yelled as she watched Andrea dig in again.

D.J.'s next pitch came whizzing right up the center of the plate and Breezy held her breath as Andrea swung. A solid hit was a great way to open an inning. But Breezy winced as she realized that Andrea had brought her bat around too late.

"Stee-rike one!" the umpire called out.

Andrea's long brown ponytail swung back and forth as she shook her head and rolled her shoulders as if to loosen up. Breezy hoped that the movement would help her teammate focus. Andrea had a tendency to dwell on strikes and forget to concentrate on the next pitch. Breezy had been working with her for the last two weeks to try to cure her of the problem.

"Focus, Andrea!" Kim called from the dugout. "Put it out of your mind!"

All that practice must have paid off, Breezy thought, as Andrea took the next pitch for a ball. It was just outside.

"Good eye!" Terry yelled. "Watch the next one!"

The next pitch didn't even need to be watched. The ball came in so low, it was practically rolling. Even though Breezy was happy that the Parrots could take advantage of D.J.'s struggles, she still felt a little sorry for him. He was normally one of the best relievers in the league — behind Chris Lavery, who played for Ten Pin Bowling. D.J. just didn't have it together that afternoon.

D.J.'s next pitch was so far outside that it almost got past the catcher. Andrea grinned at the dugout, chucked her bat, and trotted off to first.

"Way to go, girl!" Ro yelled to Andrea. "Come on, Betsy!"

Unfortunately, Betsy didn't have the eye Andrea did. She swung at the first pitch, which was up around her nose — way too high.

"Stee-rike one!" the umpire called.

"Keep your eye on it!" Breezy yelled, trying not to sound annoyed with her teammate. Betsy really had to learn to be more patient at bat, Breezy thought.

Betsy didn't even flinch as D.J.'s next pitch rocketed over the plate. D.J.'s speed was not suffering, even though his control was. Unfortunately for Betsy, the ball nicked the outside of the plate.

"Stee-rike two!"

Breezy sighed as she stepped into the on-deck circle and took a few practice swings with her bat. Then she bounced the end of the bat on the ground, sending the donut sliding down and off the bat. Bending one knee, she stretched her legs a little. She was going to need some speed and it wouldn't be good to pull a muscle — especially now.

Starting to come around on D.J.'s third pitch, Betsy checked her swing just in time. As she had guessed in the nick, the pitch was a ball. The count was now one and two.

Crossing her fingers, Breezy hoped that Betsy made it to first. Then the Parrots would have runners on first and second and Breezy would have the opportunity to bring Andrea home. Breezy really wanted to add to her total of runs batted in.

Unfortunately for Betsy, D.J. suddenly found a groove and threw a picture-perfect change-up. Betsy obviously thought she was getting a fastball and swung hard at the pitch. But she was caught off balance because the ball traveled a lot slower than a fastball, even though it looked like a fastball when the pitcher delivered it. Betsy had swung before the pitch even reached the plate.

"Stee-rike three!"

Sighing again, Breezy made sure to pat Betsy on the back as she passed. Change-ups were extremely easy to misjudge — for anybody.

Time to start playing games, Breezy thought, as she put Betsy out of her mind and focused on D.J. Although Breezy was a righthanded pitcher, she felt more comfortable batting from the left side of the plate. She dug her back foot into the dirt — hard. Then she took some mighty practice swings and glanced out at the fences rimming the outfield.

"To the moon," she muttered loud enough for Hector Martinez, the catcher, to hear.

Then Breezy fought to hide a grin as D.J. shook off Hector's signal. Breezy knew that D.J. knew that she lived for a good change-up. But his last pitch had been a change-up. It was pretty obvious that Hector was calling for one when D.J. wanted to throw a fastball. But Hector thought Breezy was swinging for the fences so the fastball would be the very last pitch D.J. should throw.

Hector must have given the same signal because D.J. tried to shake him off again.

"Time!" Hector called out loudly, as he stood up and pulled off his mask. Then he trotted out to the mound and Breezy could see that the words were really flying back and forth.

Breezy had to turn around and face her dugout because she was really going to lose it if she kept watching. She loved it when things worked out well. Hector was a formidable guy and Breezy was sure he'd get his pitch. Great. A perfect setup!

Breezy stepped back and swung her bat a couple of times — really big swings. It wouldn't hurt to play it up a little. Besides, D.J. kept glancing her way.

Finally, the catcher and pitcher came to an agreement and Hector jogged back to the plate. He crouched and Breezy stepped back into the batter's box and dug in again. She squeezed her eyes shut for a moment and wished for a change-up.

D.J. went into his windup and delivered what looked like a fastball. But it wasn't. It was a change-up!

Breezy pivoted her hips quickly as she faced D.J. and moved her left foot up next to the plate. She let the bat slide up through her left hand. As the ball reached the plate, Breezy pushed her bat into it, which made the ball travel only about four inches. She knew it was important to push the ball, not hit it.

Aiming for the third baseline, Breezy watched as the ball bounced, as if in slow motion, out to the left a few feet and then fell — dead. The change-up, if you knew it was coming, was one of the best pitches on which to bunt. It was slower, so the ball wouldn't travel too far from the bat after it made contact.

Flinging her bat behind her, Breezy took off for first as D.J. stumbled off the mound and Hector struggled to his feet. Putting her head down, Breezy put them out of her mind and drove for the base. She didn't know if they were going to throw to first, but she certainly hoped so. Since the whole point of a sacrifice bunt is to advance the runner, she definitely didn't want them throwing Andrea out at second base.

John Finnegan, Tony's first baseman, was stretched out, glove ready. The ball must be on its way, Breezy thought as her foot hit the bag. Her foot, and the ball, arrived practically at the same time. She overran the base and then turned around, waiting for the call.

It seemed like the whole field paused for a moment before the umpire yelled loudly, "Safe!"

Breezy's chest heaved as she caught her breath. She shot a grin at the dugout, where her teammates were cheering wildly.

"Come on, C.J.!" Breezy yelled as Crystal Joseph stepped up to the plate. Crystal, the Parrots first baseman, was one of those players who hadn't known anything about baseball — at all — when she joined the team. But to Breezy's surprise, Crystal had picked it up with amazing speed and was now one of the best on the team. Breezy had a hard time understanding how Crystal had learned almost everything Breezy knew from reading how-to baseball books, but she knew it was true. Of course, the eight years of ballet Crystal had taken had not hurt either.

Crystal stepped into the batter's box and stared

calmly at D.J. on the mound. Breezy grinned because she knew what the pitcher was thinking. Because of the fact that Crystal was really tall, she appeared to be an easy out — her strike zone was so big. Obviously, D.J. didn't know too much about Dave Winfield. The California Angels slugger was 6'6" tall and he was not an easy out by any stretch of the imagination.

Taking D.J.'s first pitch, Crystal dropped a blooper right over the third baseman's head. He backpedaled, but not quickly enough and everyone was safe. Bases loaded.

Breezy glanced at her best friend, Kim, as she stepped into the batter's box. It was kind of funny that the shortest girl on the team batted right after the tallest. It was probably a really shrewd move on Ro's part; it kept the pitchers off balance.

"Let's go, Kim!" Ro yelled. "Bring someone home!"

"Bring us *all* home!" Breezy added from where she stood at second base.

Kim flipped a red braid over her shoulder and pushed her batting helmet down farther on her head. Breezy knew that Kim meant business.

But D.J. picked this moment to finally show some of the stuff that made him one of the best relievers in Emblem.

His first pitch was a sinker. And it was a beautiful sinker. From her view from second, Breezy thought it must have dropped a good two to three feet right into the strike zone. Kim didn't even try to swing at it.

"Stee-rike one!" the umpire yelled as Kim stepped out of the batter's box.

Swinging her bat fiercely, Kim glared at D.J. Then she stepped back up to the plate.

Kim connected with the next pitch — a fastball on the outside. But she swung up under it, instead of level, and it popped up into short leftfield. The shortstop, Ken Fisher, just had to backpedal a few steps, raise his glove, and let the ball fall in. Two outs.

Andrea, Breezy, and Crystal hadn't budged from their bases. That was one of the first things they had all learned: if there are less than two outs when the ball is hit, never run on a fly ball that you think will be caught unless you have tagged up first. And then run only if the ball has been hit deep to the outfield. In this case, since Kim was the second out, it would have been a definite third out if one of them had tried to run. Ken Fisher had an arm like a rifle, as well as incredible accuracy.

"Come on, girl!" Ro yelled as Terry swaggered up to the plate. "Keep us alive! Don't leave any of them stranded! Let's bring some birds home!"

Terry jammed her helmet on her head and stepped into the batter's box. She glowered at D.J., who took an involuntary step back. Breezy grinned — she was going to have to get Terry to teach her the "monster look." It really worked wonders with some pitchers.

D.J. threw two wild pitches to Terry, but then seemed

to settle down. He worked the count to three balls and two strikes and then shook off Hector's last signal.

A fastball zipped right toward the plate, and Terry took a mammoth swing. She connected with a *thwack* that Breezy felt vibrate through her bones at second base. The ball rocketed in a line drive right between the first and second basemen, bringing Andrea home.

With the Parrots up 3-0, Breezy watched Liz Minters, the substitute centerfielder, step up to the plate. Liz had been injured at the beginning of the season, but Ro had added her to the roster anyway. All Breezy could say to that was, thank goodness. Liz was a consistent hitter with good power. Only Terry was stronger with the bat.

Liz took D.J.'s second pitch and blasted it deep to center. Breezy didn't even watch as the ball began to drop — there were two outs, after all — but motored for home. After she hit the plate, she spun around in time to see Crystal flying toward her.

After Crystal made it home safely, the Parrots were winning 5-0. Breezy had hoped for a cushion, but this was more like a couch! Nothing like a five-run lead to boost your confidence.

Jasmine "Jazz" Jaffe, the Parrots rightfielder and Breezy's cousin, ended the inning with three straight strikes. Breezy shook her head. Jazz would never learn how to play baseball, Breezy thought. She was more interested in the guys on the other team than in the ball flying over the plate. But at least she had stopped doing cartwheels in the outfield . . . most of the time, anyway.

Breezy dropped her helmet off in the dugout and grabbed her glove. "One inning, three outs, nine strikes," she muttered to herself as she took the field. Luckily, there had been enough action when the Parrots were up at bat to take her mind off her pitching. But now, walking out to the mound, the possibility of pitching a . . . well, one of *those* games hit her like a freight train.

Turning to face Terry when she got to the mound, Breezy slapped the ball into her glove a few times and took a deep breath. Terry gave her the thumbs up and crouched behind the plate, pointing to her mitt. Breezy knew what that meant. Focus on Terry's mitt and that was it. Don't worry about the batters or anything else. Just focus on the mitt.

Breezy threw a few easy warmups to shake out her arm. She tried to get rid of the tired feeling in her muscles. She hadn't pitched in a month, and before that she had only been pitching three innings a game. It was no wonder she was tired.

"Hey, Breeze," Ro called as she walked out to the mound. "Are you sure you want to stay in?"

Breezy opened her mouth to retort with a resounding "Yes," but Ro cut her off.

"This is a big deal, but I don't want you throwing your arm out. The game's not that important. The season is. And your arm is. I can always put Sarah in."

Breezy shook her head. She knew that Ro was only

trying to help, but she had come this far. "I have to go for it," Breezy replied. "I have to."

Ro nodded. "I understand," she said. "Go to it!" Then she turned and walked back to the dugout.

Greg Gromada was up first. Breezy watched him step into the batter's box and then turned her attention to Terry, who called for a sidearm fastball. Breezy nodded. She knew better than to shake off her catcher. Besides, that would mean that she was thinking too much, and great pitchers are not supposed to think — just throw.

"Okay, let it rip," Breezy muttered to herself as she went into her windup.

The ball left her hand and rocketed toward home. Greg's eyes widened and he swung much too late. Strike one. Breezy grinned in spite of herself — it was nice to know she was still getting some speed on the ball.

Terry called for an inside fastball to knock Greg off balance, and Breezy hummed it in there. Unfortunately, it was a little too far inside. The count was now one and one.

Breezy struggled on the next pitch, and it flew high. Two balls and one strike. Terry threw the ball back.

"Come on, Hawk," Breezy berated herself, catching the ball. "Settle down and send it up the middle."

Breezy threw an incredibly sneaky change-up and caught Greg napping. It went right up the middle of the plate and Greg didn't even twitch.

"Stee-rike two!" the umpire yelled.

"Let's go, girl!" Ro called from the dugout.

Getting the signal for a fastball, Breezy grinned. She was going to gun Greg down. Determined to put a lot of juice on the ball, she went into her windup and sent the ball flying toward the plate like it had jet engines. Greg didn't have a prayer.

"Stee-rike three!" the ump called out over the cheers of the Parrots.

"Way to go, Breezy!" Ro yelled. "Two more. You can do it."

Terry grinned at Breezy and held up two fingers.

Breezy shook out her arm and faced Ken Fisher, the next batter. He crouched really low to shorten his strike zone.

Terry called for a sinker, and Breezy put what she had on it. But it was too much — the ball dropped down below Ken's knees.

"Ball one!"

Feeling her control slipping, Breezy gave herself a mental shake to try to hang on. Her next pitch, though, brushed Ken back out of the batter's box. The ball just wasn't going where she wanted it to.

"Concentrate, Breezy!" Crystal called from first. "Concentrate on Terry's mitt."

But her next two pitches weren't anywhere near Terry's mitt, or the plate for that matter. Breezy pulled her hat off in disgust. She couldn't believe she had just walked Ken. What a giveaway. There was nothing worse than a base on balls to throw a pitcher off balance.

"Get back in the groove," Breezy mumbled to herself, jamming her hat back on her head.

John Finnegan glared back at her from the plate. Breezy narrowed her eyes at him. John was one of the guys in Emblem who hated girls playing baseball, and he really hated it when they beat him.

"Come on, babe," John taunted. "Give me what you've got! I'll give it right back to you!"

Breezy felt a new resolve building and knew she had to do everything possible to get him out. The game, and even her pitching, suddenly took the back burner. This was personal.

Zipping three straight, very fast strikes by John, Breezy didn't even realize that she had gotten her second out until Ro yelled, "Only one more!"

Breezy watched as Hector Martinez stalked, ever so slowly, to the plate. If anyone could break up what she had going, it was the dude looking at her.

"It's just like any other out," Breezy said to herself. "You can do it. Focus. Focus."

Breezy's control was definitely slipping now, and the ball was no longer going where she aimed it. Struggling, Breezy worked the count to three and two. And then it was down to one last pitch. This was it. If she walked Hector, Breezy really didn't know if she had enough left in her arm to even pitch to one more batter.

"Time!" Terry suddenly called out and trotted out to

the mound. Breezy watched her approach, feeling a little annoyed. She wanted to get this over with.

"Breeze, how ya' doing?" Terry asked, blowing a major bubble and then snapping her gum.

Breezy nodded grimly. She was trying so hard to focus that she was afraid to smile. She might lose her concentration.

"Relax," Terry continued. "It's just a stupid game, right? We've pretty much got it sewn up. And it's just one pitch. Don't even think about it. Just blast it in!"

And with that, the Parrots catcher turned and headed back to her position behind home plate. Breezy walked to the back of the mound and took off her glove. She put it under her arm and pulled off her hat. Tightening the rubber band in her ponytail, Breezy took a deep breath and stared at her cleats for a moment.

"Get this game moving, Hawk!" Kim called from her position at shortstop.

Breezy's head snapped up to see her best friend's freckled face grinning at her.

"Just strike him out so we can go get something to eat!" Kim continued. "I'm starvin', Marvin."

How could Kim be hungry at a time like this, Breezy wondered. This was a major turning point in her baseball career, and Kim was worried about her stomach? Then Breezy grinned at her friend. Kim was always hungry.

Still smiling, Breezy put her hat and glove back on and climbed back up onto the mound. She stepped on the rubber, faced Terry, took the signal for a sidearm fastball, and went into her windup.

It was super slow mo' as Breezy watched the ball leave her hand and travel toward the plate. She held her breath, waiting for the thump of the ball as it hit Terry's mitt. It never came.

Hector swung late, but managed to connect. The ball hit his bat and rocketed out to the infield in a head-high line drive — right at Kim.

And suddenly, everything sped up again. Breezy felt as if she couldn't watch, but she couldn't drag her eyes away from Kim. Kim threw her glove up in front of her face. The ball sailed right in and Kim closed her glove around it.

"Hey!" Kim exclaimed, looking really surprised. "I got it. I got it! He's out! You did it, Breeze!"

Breezy stood on the mound with a major smile plastered on her face. She couldn't move. She just couldn't move. But she had done it! She had really done it! She pitched a no-hitter!

That was her last clear thought before she was tackled by the entire team.

2

"Here she is!" Kim called out the next morning at school. "The famous Breezy Hawk!"

Breezy grinned and walked over to where her best friend was standing. "Hey, Kim," she said, opening her locker. "What's going on?"

Kim choked. "What's going on?" she asked in shock. "Breeze, I saw you on the news last night. On television! I couldn't believe it! Didn't you see it?"

"Oh, yeah," Breezy admitted. "I did. But I didn't think anyone else had seen it."

"Yo!" Terry DiSunno yelled from the other end of the hall. "It's Emblem's answer to Nolan Ryan!"

Breezy flushed a little and watched Terry stride toward her. She hadn't expected anyone else to have seen the news. Who watched the news anyway? All this attention was kind of taking her by surprise.

"Way to go, Breeze!" Terry exclaimed, patting Breezy on the back. "Television coverage already! You're definitely going places."

"Guys, I was on for less than ten seconds," Breezy protested. This was getting a little out of control.

"You're a star!" Terry exclaimed.

"Come on," Breezy protested. "I couldn't have done anything without the team. The Parrots are the real stars here."

"Did you see the article on the front page of *The Hampstead Times* this morning?" Crystal asked, coming up behind them. She waved a newspaper in front of Breezy. "It's even got a huge picture. You're a celebrity!"

Breezy blinked as she stared at a large photograph of herself on the pitcher's mound. She knew that no one had ever pitched a no-hitter in Emblem before, but it wasn't like she had thrown a perfect game or anything. In a perfect game, the pitcher doesn't give up any hits or walks.

Eyes narrowing, Breezy read the headline: GIRL PITCHER THROWS NO-HITTER. "What difference does it make that I'm a girl?" she asked her teammates angrily. Maybe she was only getting all this press because she was a girl!

"Let me see!" Kim demanded, grabbing the paper from her friend. "Oh, snap! That's terrible."

"Maybe you should write a letter to the editor," Crystal suggested seriously.

"Maybe I will," Breezy replied.

Just then the warning bell rang for homeroom.

"Guys, we better motor or we'll be late for class,"

Terry announced as she started walking away. "I'll see you at lunch, okay?" Then she grinned back at Breezy. "If you can escape the autograph hounds, that is."

Breezy laughed. "Right," she called out. "I'll sign them 'Girl Pitcher.'"

Grabbing her books, Breezy slammed her locker shut and took off for class.

The morning flew by. It seemed as if the whole school had watched the news or read that morning's paper. Everyone kept congratulating her. Breezy was shocked when Mr. Delany, her science teacher, who had never said two words to her outside of the classroom, made the entire class give her a round of applause. Talk about embarrassing.

Finally, it was time for lunch. Breezy went back to her locker to pick up her lunch bag and drop off her books. She kind of wished that she could eat at home or some-thing — all this attention was beginning to get to her and she wanted some space. Even the principal had made an announcement over the loudspeaker about her no-hitter! It was totally unreal.

She wondered if this was how Cal Ripken, Junior, the All-Star shortstop for the Baltimore Orioles, felt every time he went out shopping or went wherever in Balti-more. The news always showed him being followed by hordes of fans. She had no idea how he took it.

"I'll meet you in the caf," someone called out behind Breezy and then bumped right into her.

Breezy spun around and found herself face-to-face with Lindsay Cunningham. Lindsay flipped her long, white blonde hair over her shoulder and sneered at Breezy.

"Well, if it isn't the little tomboy," Lindsay said.

Breezy smiled. It was the first time all day that she was truly happy about the publicity she had gotten. It was probably totally killing Lindsay. Lindsay considered herself just about the most popular thing this side of Madonna. Breezy thought she was an airhead who probably wouldn't even sneeze without her boyfriend's permission. Besides, she didn't know a fly ball from a house fly.

"Hey, Lindsay," Breezy replied in a friendly tone of voice.

Lindsay looked shocked, and Breezy smiled again. Breezy didn't think she had ever spoken to Ms. Cunningham nicely before.

"Please try not to bump my pitching arm," Breezy continued. "It's like a million-dollar arm. And it's Eleanor Roosevelt Junior High's most valuable asset. Just ask the principal."

Narrowing her eyes, Lindsay flipped her hair over her shoulder again and started to walk away from Breezy.

"I'd offer you my autograph, but it really isn't worth straining my arm, you know what I mean?" Breezy called loudly after Lindsay.

Lindsay didn't turn around, but just walked faster as

if she couldn't wait to get away from Breezy. Breezy cracked up watching Lindsay hurry off. She was laughing so hard, she actually started to cry a little. Being the center of attention had been worth it just to see Lindsay's face. She looked like she was about to have a cow.

"What's the matter, Breeze?" Kim asked, tapping her friend on the shoulder.

Breezy wiped the tears off her face. "I just offered my autograph to Lindsay Cunningham," she said, starting to laugh again.

"No way!" Kim exclaimed, giggling. "She must have died! That's hysterical."

"It was great," Breezy admitted. "I'm Marvin. Let's jam to the *caf*." She laughed and flipped her ponytail over her shoulder, mimicking Lindsay. That girl really was too much, Breezy thought.

"Sounds good!" Kim agreed as the two girls took off in the same direction as Lindsay.

"Hey, Breezy!" someone called out as Kim and Breezy scanned the crowded cafeteria for a table. "Over here!"

Breezy searched for the owner of the voice and spotted Terry standing up near the team's table. She didn't know how, or even when, it had happened, but the Parrots had all started eating lunch together. Breezy thought that was a really good thing for the team. And as captain, she tried to maintain that feeling of unity.

"Oops, forgot a straw," Breezy said, looking down at her tray. "I'll meet you over there."

24

Kim walked over to the table and Breezy turned to go back to the condiment table.

"Hi, Breezy," Peter Tolhurst said as she grabbed a straw.

"Oh . . . uh, hi, Peter," Breezy replied, feeling her face get a little flushed. Sometimes she didn't know what to say when she talked to Peter. She hadn't felt like that last year. After all, Peter was the best slugger in Emblem — not to mention an awesome basketball player — and Breezy loved talking sports with anyone.

But then, at the beginning of the season, Kim had mentioned that she was sure that Peter *liked* Breezy. And now that Kim had said that, Breezy became really self-conscious when she saw Peter. They still had a good time when they were together. But they didn't go out on dates or anything. Well, there was the time they had gone to the Neptune Diner together — but that was after a game. And then there was the time at the Spring Fling Dance — but it wasn't as if they came together or left together or anything. So neither of them really counted as dates. Just thinking about the whole situation confused Breezy.

"Well, Breezy?" Peter asked a little loudly.

"Well what?" Breezy asked, blankly. She shook her head slightly to clear it. What was she doing thinking about guys? She was being as bad as her cousin Jazz and she was nothing like her cousin.

"So Breeze, how does it feel to be a pitching phenom?" Peter asked, grinning at her.

"It's a little embarrassing," Breezy admitted for the first time all day.

"Yeah, well, I heard you offered an autograph to Lindsay," Peter replied, laughing. "She was mighty miffed. I don't think Joey was too pleased, either." Joey Carpenter was Lindsay's on-again-off-again boyfriend and no particular favorite of Breezy's.

Breezy laughed. "News travels fast at Roosevelt! Anyway, I don't understand why she looked so upset," she said jokingly. "I mean, something like that might be worth money some day."

"True, true," Peter said, suddenly sounding serious. "You never know."

"Well, if it isn't Little Miss Publicity," Joey Carpenter interrupted sarcastically.

Breezy turned to face him, her hands on her hips. She wasn't about to take anything from him. She hadn't asked to be on the news or the front page.

"Is it my fault I'm a better pitcher than you?" Breezy retorted, taking a step toward Joey. Peter put his hand on her shoulder, holding her back.

Joey's top lip curled up in a sneer. "That will be the day," he said laughing, as he grinned at the group of guys that always seemed to surround him. John Richie patted him on the back.

"Right," Breezy agreed. "That's why I'm in the papers and you're in third place."

It was true, too. Joey's team, Mitchell Lumber, was

indeed in third place — behind Mel's Auto Body and the Pink Parrots. And Breezy loved every minute of it. Joey and his father, Coach Carpenter, really believed that girls couldn't play baseball. There was nothing like beating them to prove them wrong.

Joey clenched his fists and moved toward Breezy.

"Hey, hey," Peter suddenly said, stepping in between Breezy and Joey. "Why don't you just drop it, Carpenter. She pitched a no-hitter. A *no-hitter*. Have you ever done that?"

Joey shifted uncomfortably and broke Peter's gaze to look over at his buddies. Breezy couldn't believe it. This was the closest Breezy had seen Joey come to actually admitting that she had done something he hadn't!

The last time Joey backed down because of Peter, Breezy had told Crystal all about it, not believing it. Crystal had said that Joey probably didn't want Peter mad at him. Peter was, after all, the most popular boy in the school, and he even knew a lot of high school kids. And then there was the fact that Peter was such an incredible athlete. Breezy didn't think that Joey cared about anybody else, but she had been wrong before. And Crystal was usually right about things like this.

Joey gave Breezy one more glare and then spun around and walked away. His friends all followed him.

"You shouldn't let him get to you like that," Peter said, turning back to Breezy.

"Well, he makes me so mad!" Breezy retorted.

"That's what he wants to do," Peter replied calmly, picking up Breezy's tray. "Come on, Miss No-Hitter. I'll walk you over to your adoring teammates."

Breezy stood there motionless for a moment, her mouth hanging open, watching Peter walk away. There was just no figuring the guy out. She shook her head and followed him.

3

"Okay, birds!" Ro called out Friday afternoon. "Settle down. I've got an announcement to make."

Breezy grinned. She had an announcement to make as well.

The Pink Parrots had all gathered at the Neptune Diner after practice. Jazz's parents owned the diner and the Parrots spent a lot of time there. They couldn't really agree whether it was the food or the service that kept them coming back. Breezy definitely loved the milk shakes, but she knew a lot of the Parrots kept coming back because of Eddie Andrews.

Eddie worked at the diner most afternoons. He was studying law enforcement and wanted to go to the state trooper academy. In his mid-20s, he had short, curly black hair and hazel eyes that Jazz said were "to die for." And he was into bodybuilding.

All the Parrots were convinced that he and Ro kind of had a thing for each other. But as far as Breezy knew, they had never gone on a date or anything. Eddie had come to a bunch of their games, though.

"Birds!" Ro called again, standing up.

Looking at Ro, Breezy shook her head. The Parrots coach was wearing leopard print biker shorts and a cropped black and gold T-shirt. Her brown curly hair was, of course, hairsprayed at least three inches above her scalp. With her long gold fingernails and bright makeup, Ro definitely didn't look as if she had just led the Parrots through a rigorous workout. But she had. In fact, she always did all the exercises and drills she made her team do. And while everyone else was gasping and panting for breath, Ro was bouncing around, singing and dancing all over the field. Unbelievable, Breezy thought.

"Yo!" Breezy called out loudly, trying to help out her coach. Spirits were pretty high, and Breezy knew that the Parrots were still psyched about her no-hitter and all the publicity they were getting. She grinned, almost unable to hold in her news any longer. The team was going to die when she told them. But Ro had an announcement first — and she was the coach after all.

Everyone quieted down pretty quickly then.

"As you know," Ro began, pacing back and forth between the two booths where the Parrots were sitting, "the All-Star Game is quickly approaching. This year, the matchup is going to take place in Baltimore."

Ro paused for a moment. "Where the Baltimore Orioles play," she continued, grinning at the girls.

A chance to play in a major league ballpark, Breezy thought excitedly. That was totally awesome! The All-Star Game was usually kind of a big deal — Emblem against Wemble (the Western Maryland Baseball League). But it had never been *this* big.

It was funny, but even though she hadn't made the All-Star team the year before, Breezy knew that she was a definite shoo-in this year. No question. How could they not pick the only no-hitter pitcher in the league?

"So, this year two Parrots have been honored," Ro went on and then paused and stared at all the girls.

Breezy moved forward to the edge of the booth bench impatiently. She knew she was going to be picked, and she just wished Ro would get on with it already. Enough of the dramatics.

"The slugging sensation, Terry DiSunno, and our very own no-hitter hurler, Breezy Hawk!" Ro finally said.

Sitting back with a satisfied smile, Breezy wondered why she had been even a little nervous. There was no question about her being chosen. *The Hampstead Times* would have kicked up quite a fuss if she hadn't. She was still all over the sports pages, two days after throwing her no-hitter.

It was really nice to finally get some attention for her pitching. Breezy had known last year that she was a good pitcher, but Coach Carpenter never, ever put her in a game last year. She had been frustrated all season. And it just wasn't fair. Why should it matter that she was a girl? But that was all history now. Sure, she had gotten mad about that headline in the paper the day before, but she had made the front page. And it wasn't as if she lived for the press or anything, because she didn't. Breezy had to admit, though, that she was starting to enjoy the publicity a little — it gave her a chance to put those guys who thought girls couldn't play baseball right in their places. And she had gotten picked for the All-Star team! You couldn't really beat that.

"Congratulations, girls," Ro finished. "I want to rent a van to take the rest of the team to watch you two beat Wemble single-handedly."

"Cool!" Kim exclaimed as Eddie called Ro over to the counter.

Jazz raised her eyebrows at everyone as soon as Ro walked away. "I'd love to be a bridesmaid in their wedding," she said, looking from Eddie and Ro to the Parrots and back again.

"Don't you think that's rushing things just a bit?" Terry asked. "I mean, they haven't even gone on a real date yet."

"Well, sometimes in matters of the heart, you don't need to go on dates," Jazz replied. "You just know."

Terry laughed. "Sure," she said, agreeing with Jazz. "Just like you know when you're hungry or thirsty, right?"

"It's more romantic than that, Ter!" Jazz protested.

"Hey, so you guys are going to play against the Baltimore Orioles? Do you think that's a good idea? Don't you think they'll win?" she asked, changing the subject.

Terry laughed as Breezy winced. How Terry could put up with her cousin sometimes was totally beyond Breezy. Jazz knew nothing about baseball — and she didn't even care. Breezy had little patience with her. But Terry and Jazz were best friends.

"No, Jazz," Terry answered, still laughing. "We would never win against the Orioles in a million years. But we don't play the Orioles."

"You don't?" Jazz asked, sounding more confused. "Then why are you playing in their stadium?"

"Because it's a really big deal," Breezy answered brusquely. "You know, the very best baseball players in Maryland playing against each other is pretty major. It's practically the highlight of the season."

"I think the playoffs are pretty important, too," Kim added. "The best teams going against each other is big time."

"Yeah, but not everyone on the playoff teams is a star," Breezy stated flatly, slurping up the last of her chocolate milk shake.

"They're both pretty important," Crystal cut in. "I don't think you can really compare them either, since they're so different."

What was Crystal talking about, Breezy wondered. Of course you could. She just had. Not that it wouldn't be cool if the Parrots won the playoffs, but she would know that some of the players on the team were just better than others. Now, in the All-Star Game, all the players would pull more than their own weight. The players chosen were the "heavyweights" of Emblem.

"You guys won't believe this!" Breezy exclaimed, suddenly remembering her incredible news. "WXRK, you know, Channel Four, wants to do a segment on me for the national network. Isn't that wild?"

"That's great, Breeze!" Kim replied. "When are they going to do it?"

"We should tape it," Terry added. "You know, use it for recruiting next season or something."

"Recruiting?" Jazz asked. "What do we have to recruit?"

"More players," Betsy answered. "We could be huge."

"I don't know," Kim said. "I think we've got enough people now, don't you?"

"Yeah," Terry responded. "I mean, we all joined the Parrots so we could actually play. If we have too many players, that could really cut into everyone's playing time." She reached over and snagged one of Jazz's french fries. "It was just a suggestion."

Breezy fumed silently. She couldn't believe the Parrots were talking about recruitment when she had just told them she was going to be on national television. What was wrong with them? This was a big deal.

"About this segment," Crystal began slowly.

Thank goodness, Breezy thought. Finally, someone saw the importance of this event. She sat up a little straighter — she was sure professional baseball players didn't have poor posture. Besides, Breezy didn't want to be slouching on television when she was interviewed. She nodded at Crystal.

"The network's not . . . uh . . . not going to use the 'girl pitcher' angle, is it?" Crystal asked hesitantly.

In shock for a moment, Breezy stared at Crystal in disbelief. "What are you talking about?" she asked a little shortly. "What difference does it make? I'm going to be on national television."

"I guess it doesn't really," Crystal said, backing down a little.

"Of course it makes a difference!" Terry put in firmly. "You said yourself, Breezy, that it shouldn't matter that you're a girl. If these guys are only doing this show because you're a girl, then maybe you should protest or something and not tape it."

"Really," Kim agreed. "I mean, if a guy had thrown a no-hitter, would he get the same coverage? The whole point behind the Parrots is that we proved we're as good as guys. So why sell out now?"

"I'm not selling out!" Breezy protested. "I can't believe you can even say that. *I* started this team, remember?" she asked, practically yelling now.

Breezy could not believe the way her teammates were

acting. It was like they didn't want her to be on television or something. But there was no way they could stop her. "I am *going* to be on television," she announced. "You know, I think you guys are just jealous or something. You obviously can't handle the fact that I'm getting all this publicity and the rest of the team is not getting anything. Can I help it if I'm a good pitcher?"

Breezy looked at the shocked faces of her teammates and stood up. They were probably just upset that she had figured out what was going on. But she didn't really care. It wasn't as if she needed their approval to do this news segment anyway. They were just going to have to live with it. Besides, she had carried her teammates long enough — it was time they gave something back to her. And she wanted a little more enthusiasm. They would never make it without her, and they should realize that. Breezy was just asking for what she deserved. She threw some money on the table for her milk shake and stood up.

"See ya'," she called over her shoulder as she marched out of the diner. If the Parrots weren't going to be happy for her, and if they were going to act all jealous, then Breezy really didn't think she wanted to hang out with them anymore. Why couldn't they understand? Why did they have to make things so difficult?

4

"Now, just have a seat, little lady," Melvin Myers said to Breezy the following afternoon.

Melvin Myers definitely looked a lot older in person than he did on television, Breezy decided. She and her mother had come down to Baltimore for the interview part of the national television segment.

Breezy sat on the edge of the sofa in the Channel Four waiting room and studied Melvin Myers. She had watched him on WXRK for as long as she could remember. He was a great sports anchor, and he got a lot of sports stars on the show. Somehow, though, Breezy hadn't expected him to be wearing so much makeup. And his hair looked like Ro's: sparkly and stiff.

"She couldn't have worn a dress?" Melvin Myers asked Mrs. Hawk loudly.

Breezy's mom shot her a look and raised her eyebrows. Breezy couldn't understand why Melvin Myers was talking as if she wasn't in the same room with him. She had a mouth and could have answered that question easily, no matter how dumb it had been.

"What's wrong with what I'm wearing?" Breezy asked Melvin Myers just as loudly. She had felt pretty professional that morning when she put on her pleated khaki linen shorts, white, khaki, and black checked vest and white T-shirt. Breezy pointed her toes and looked down at her new black patent leather flats. What did this guy expect, Breezy wondered. A ball gown?

"Well, she just looks a little too . . . too . . . sporty," Melvin Myers answered Mrs. Hawk — not Breezy. Breezy started a slow boil. This guy was really getting her mad. "You know, I wanted her more feminine. Like a *real* little girl."

"She is a real girl," Mrs. Hawk replied pointedly. Score one for Mom, Breezy thought, grinning. "Besides, I think she looks great the way she is."

"Yeah, sure," Melvin Myers said hastily. "I didn't say she didn't. She looks fine. Well, maybe if we do something about that hair it will help."

Breezy patted her French braid as the sports anchor ushered them down the hallway. What were they going to do with her hair? She liked it just the way it was. Her mother had braided it for her that morning.

Opening a door marked MAKEUP, Melvin Myers motioned for Breezy and her mother to step inside. Breezy stopped short in the doorway when she saw what was in the room. There were wall-to-wall mirrors with swivel chairs in front of them that looked like the ones in her dentist's office. Actually, Breezy realized that the room really reminded her of the Pink Parrot, Ro's beauty salon. Bottles of goop, cans of hairspray, jars of makeup, and brushes were all over the counters. A balding man with a long ponytail, who was dressed all in black, turned toward them. He held a large makeup brush in his hand.

"No way, Mom," Breezy said, shaking her head. "I'm not going in there. This place is scary."

Mrs. Hawk put her arm around Breezy's shoulders.

"What's the problem?" Melvin Myers asked impatiently. "We've got a lot of work to do before we go before the cameras."

"Definitely," the man in black agreed, walking toward Breezy.

Breezy took a step back and bumped right into Melvin Myers. He gave her a little push and propelled her into the makeup room.

"I'm Victor," the makeup man continued. "Sit down. We don't have much time."

Feeling as if she was going to meet the firing squad or something, Breezy took a deep breath and moved slowly toward one of the swivel chairs.

"You know what to do, Victor," Melvin Myers said. "Go for the look we talked about. I'll be back in ten. Mrs. Hawk, could you come with me for a few minutes? I've got some papers you need to sign." And with that, he was gone.

Looking helplessly at her mom, Breezy wished that she didn't have to be left alone — with Victor.

"I'll be back soon, Amy," Mrs. Hawk said, following Melvin Myers into the hallway. Breezy's mother was the only person who called her daughter by her real name, Amy. "Don't worry about anything."

Breezy stared at herself in the mirror, as the door shut behind her mother. Victor started to unbraid her hair.

"What are you doing?" Breezy asked, jerking her head away. "I like my hair like this."

Victor sighed. "Melvin Myers wants you to look more feminine," he said slowly. "So your hair must be softer. You don't want to look like a little tomboy on television, do you?" he asked and then chuckled as if there was no question about the answer. "Please cooperate."

With one last glare, Breezy sat back in her chair. She didn't like the direction this whole thing seemed to be taking, but she had no idea what to do about it. It seemed as if things really were turning out the way her friends had thought. Maybe they were right. Maybe she should have boycotted the interview. But how was she supposed to know? Besides, how could she pass up the opportunity to be on national television?

After one last protest, Breezy shut her eyes as Victor reached for a jar of green goop. She definitely didn't want to see what he was doing to her, even though he had silenced her with a promise that her makeup would be subtle when it was finished. She couldn't wait until this whole TV interview thing was over. At this point, she didn't think she had much choice about it anyway.

Ten minutes later, the door opened and shut.

"That's more like it," Melvin Myers said as Breezy's eyes popped open.

She was about to ask where her mother was but stopped as she saw her reflection in one of the mirrors.

"What did you do to me?" Breezy asked in shock. "I barely recognize myself."

Breezy's hair was loose and full, falling down around her shoulders in soft waves. Victor had hairsprayed it up a few inches on top of her head. Putting her hand up to touch it, Breezy gasped. Her hair felt like plastic or something. And the makeup was anything but subtle! Victor had applied light brown eyeshadow, pinkish lipstick, and some beige stuff all over her face. Breezy felt as if she were wearing a mask.

"Yes, isn't it incredible?" Victor exclaimed, enthusiastically.

"*Now* you look like a real little lady," Melvin Myers said with a satisfied smile on his face. Looking Breezy up and down slowly, Melvin gave Victor a brief nod. He sat down in the other swivel chair. "Your mother will be joining us in the studio."

Breezy wanted to set him straight about this *little lady* stuff, but she just couldn't seem to find the words. Known for her quick comebacks, Breezy had rarely had this problem.

Victor left her sitting there, mouth agape, and took his makeup brush over to Melvin Myers' chair. Breezy watched, fascinated, as Victor covered the sports anchor's face with makeup. She never knew that men wore that much makeup — even on television.

Stifling a giggle, Breezy could not believe it when Victor lifted the top of Melvin Myers' hair. A toupee?! Melvin Myers wore a toupee? Breezy couldn't wait to tell Kim. Then she remembered she wasn't really talking to Kim. She wished her mother was there to see this, at least.

Victor brushed some sticky stuff on the underside of Melvin Myers' toupee and patted it back on his head.

"What?" Melvin Myers demanded, staring at Breezy.

Breezy just shook her head, trying very hard not to laugh. She didn't really think Melvin Myers would appreciate that.

Five minutes later, Victor was finished with both of them. Melvin Myers stood up, nodded at the makeup man, and said to Breezy, "Let's go. It's show time."

Standing up, Breezy tried not to look at her reflection. Of course, it was difficult since the room was wall-to-wall mirrors. But she really didn't want to see what she looked like. Everything the Parrots had said at the diner kept running through her mind. They were right and she didn't want to find out how right they were.

As Breezy trotted down the hallway after Melvin Myers, she gritted her teeth in determination. Even though they had changed the way she looked, they couldn't change her. She might look as if she'd bought into that whole "girl pitcher" thing. But she hadn't. And she would just have to make sure that the television audience knew that.

They turned a corner, Melvin Myers opened a door, and suddenly they were in the actual television studio. Breezy heard a gasp and turned to see her mother staring at her with her mouth open.

"What did they do to you?" Mrs. Hawk asked, her eyes darting to Melvin Myers' back and then narrowing. "You don't look like yourself."

"I know, Mom," Breezy agreed. "I couldn't stop that guy, though. He wouldn't listen to me. I feel like Jazz."

"You do kind of look like her," Breezy's mother admitted.

"Great," Breezy muttered. "Here I am, appearing on national television, looking like my ditzy cousin."

"Come here, honey," Melvin Myers called out. He had walked over to a group of chairs, rimmed by lights, in the center of the studio.

Breezy frowned at her mother. She hated being called honey, or dear, or anything like that. She suspected that Melvin Myers couldn't remember her name.

"You know, Amy," her mother said quickly, brushing some of Breezy's hair out of her eyes. "My goodness, your hair is stiff. What did they put in it, glue?"

Breezy giggled. It certainly felt like it.

"But seriously," Mrs. Hawk began again, "you don't

have to do this. If you're not comfortable here, or with this," she said gesturing to Breezy's hair, "then we'll just go home. It's no skin off my nose — or yours either."

Breezy nodded. "I know, Mom," she answered. A large part of her just wanted to turn around and walk right out of the studio. Of course, she'd have to tell Melvin Myers a thing or two before she left — like her name. She was more than just a "little lady" or a "girl pitcher," and she wanted him to know it. She was an athlete, and a darn good one, and she deserved more respect than this. Somehow, Breezy didn't think Melvin Myers would call Martina Navratilova a "little lady."

But, she reminded herself, this was national television, after all. She had thrown a no-hitter and had every reason to be in this studio. So they had some strange ideas about the way she ought to look. Big deal. She could deal with that, and straighten them out about the "girls and sports" stuff at the same time.

"It's okay," Breezy said firmly. "I want to do this."

"We're waiting for you, hon!" Melvin Myers called.

"Do you have a tissue, Mom?" Breezy asked, holding out her hand. Her mother looked at her questioningly, but dug into her pocket and pulled out her handkerchief. Breezy took it and wiped off her lipstick. She was going to do this interview all right — but not as a "little lady."

5

"Breeze! Breeze!" Breezy's nine-year-old brother, Danny, screamed loudly.

Breezy squeezed her eyes shut more tightly and burrowed down farther under her covers. Maybe if she just ignored him, he would go away.

"Get up, Breeze!" Danny shouted again, even louder this time.

Hearing the door of her room open, Breezy tried to lay as still as possible. If Danny thought she was asleep, he might leave her alone.

"Breezy, you can't stay in bed forever, you know," Danny went on matter-of-factly, sitting down on the edge of her bed. "You have to get up and go to school."

"Why?" Breezy mumbled, still not opening her eyes.

Danny paused for a minute, and Breezy hoped that there was no good reason why she had to get out of bed. "Mom says," he finally answered.

Groaning, Breezy figured that was a pretty good reason. Even though her mother was sort of laid-back most of the time, she still meant what she said.

"All right, all right," Breezy replied, finally opening her eyes.

"Come on, Breeze," Danny said, grinning. "It's not that bad. I thought you looked pretty on television."

Breezy groaned again and buried her head under her pillow. The interview. It had aired on television last night on the Sunday night seven o'clock news. Breezy thought it had probably been the worst five minutes of her life.

Despite her determination to come across as a serious athlete, Breezy knew she had looked like a total ditz instead — worse than Jazz ever had. Every time Breezy had brought up the subject of baseball, swimming, or other sports, Melvin Myers had asked her about boys. He wanted to know if she had a boyfriend. Then he went on and on about how he thought Breezy should be worried about boys' reactions to her beating them. He said straight out that boys don't like girls who play better than they do. He even wanted to know if she was worried about breaking her fingernails when she played.

Breezy grimaced thinking about the worst part of it. Even worse than coming off as an empty-headed bingo-brain was the fact that the studio had edited out everything she had said about the rest of the Parrots and Ro. Breezy had stressed the fact that she couldn't have pitched a no-hitter without the support of her teammates and coach. And she had told Melvin Myers that the team was really important to her and other stuff like that. But none of that had been part of the clip that aired on television last night.

Melvin Myers had done almost all of the talking in the segment. The few parts that had been left in when Breezy was speaking, were the ones in which she had only talked about herself. She sounded like a total egomaniac. But a lot of it was because so many of her quotes were taken completely out of context.

And Danny thought she looked pretty. Great. She was sure that even Lindsay Cunningham would have come off better in an interview than she had. Breezy grinned for a minute. Lindsay would probably do really well with Melvin Myers. She would probably love being called a little lady and being asked about her fingernails.

That thought wasn't enough to keep her in a good mood, though. After she kicked Danny out of her room, Breezy finally got up. She threw on jeans and a T-shirt and went down to breakfast.

"Morning," Breezy mumbled, sitting down at the kitchen table. She looked at the bowl of cereal in front of her, not wanting to talk to anyone.

"Hey, Breeze," Russ, Breezy's 15-year-old brother, greeted her — a little too enthusiastically, Breezy thought.

"Don't worry about it," Tom said, patting Breezy on the shoulder. Breezy sometimes felt her 16-year-old brother tried too hard to be the voice of experience. How could she not worry about this? It was a major problem.

"I'm sure not too many kids saw the news last night anyway," Mr. Hawk added, sitting down with a huge stack of pancakes.

"That's true," Mrs. Hawk agreed, pouring Breezy's orange juice.

"Well . . ." Danny said, and then trailed off.

"What?" Breezy asked shortly, raising her head and eyeing her younger brother.

"Well, I guess I kind of told Jazz and everybody yesterday afternoon at the diner to make sure and watch you at seven o'clock last night," Danny admitted.

Breezy glared at him. Great, she thought. Now all of the Parrots were sure to have seen her sounding like a braggart with nothing between her ears. Terrific.

"I'm sorry, Breeze," Danny apologized, his blue eyes wide. "I didn't mean it."

Softening, Breezy tried to smile at her brother. It almost worked. "It's okay, Danny," she said. "It's not your fault the interview was so terrible. Don't worry about it."

Breakfast was over much too quickly, and before she knew it, Breezy was riding her bike to school. It was a ride of dread, she thought. She tried pedaling really slowly, but it didn't help. The brick facade of Eleanor Roosevelt Junior High was in front of her in a matter of minutes.

Breezy locked her bike up at the bike rack and headed into school, hoping she wouldn't see anyone she knew.

This was going to be the worst day of her life — she just knew it.

If only Kim had called her last night. Then Breezy could have told her that the Parrots had all been right about that interview. And then she wouldn't have to worry about today because the Parrots would still be with her.

But it wasn't her fault that the segment had been edited the way it was. She *had* mentioned the Parrots — repeatedly. Breezy wasn't self-centered and big-headed. And if her team didn't know that about her by now, and if they didn't know that she knew that she couldn't have thrown a no-hitter without them, then nothing she could say now would change that. Besides, if they didn't know how much the Parrots meant to her, than they didn't know her very well.

Breezy stiffened her spine and walked up the front steps to school. She wasn't going to let anything upset her.

Walking into the front hall, Breezy saw Terry, Jazz, Kim, and Crystal standing by Terry's locker.

"Hi, guys," Breezy said, walking up to them. "What's going on?"

Terry's green eyes flashed angrily at Breezy. She didn't say anything — just stared at her for a minute and then began rummaging in her locker as if Breezy wasn't even there.

Breezy looked at the other three girls. Jazz wouldn't

meet her eyes, but stared at her pink sneakers instead as if they were the most interesting thing in the world. Crystal looked at a point on the wall right beyond Breezy's right ear. Kim was the only one who met her gaze.

"Well, Kim?" Breezy asked a little shortly. This was some treatment, she thought. It was great how her friends stood by her. They had already judged her without even waiting to hear about what had really happened.

Kim looked at the other three girls and then she looked back at Breezy. "We saw you on television last night, Breezy," she said softly.

"Oh, yeah?" Breezy questioned, her dark eyes blazing. What was she supposed to say to that now? That they were totally right? Or maybe she should tell them how Melvin Myers had treated her? Or how they had edited out just about everything she said?

"I can't believe you let them do that to your hair," Kim replied, meeting her best friend's gaze squarely. "They really did the whole 'girl pitcher' thing, didn't they? And we really did warn you. How could you have sold out?"

Breezy was suddenly really angry. She couldn't remember the last time she had been this mad — maybe when she quit Mitchell Lumber and told Coach Carpenter off. She didn't know. But it was just terrific the way her friends wanted to hear her side of it.

"You all think I sold out?" Breezy asked, practically

spitting out the words. She looked at Jazz and Crystal — Terry was still facing her locker. Both of them looked right at the floor. "Do you?" Breezy insisted.

Both of them nodded slightly.

"Just great," Breezy muttered, totally furious.

"It was really nice of you to mention your team-mates!" Terry exclaimed, turning around. "We really appreciate it. I mean, you can't thank us in public because you did it all on your own, right?"

That was it for Breezy. The last straw. Her own team-mates — her friends — thought she was an egomaniac. She would have expected it from Lindsay and her clones, but not from her own friends. That really hurt.

"Last time I checked," Breezy began, wanting to hurt them back, "no one else on the team pitched a no-hitter. Can I help it if I've got more talent than anyone else?"

Breezy didn't wait for an answer, but spun on her heel and walked down the hall toward her locker. She had to get away. She was really angry — and she definitely didn't want them to see how upset and hurt she was, too.

6

"Hey, Breeze," Peter Tolhurst called to Breezy the following afternoon. It was their first All-Star practice and Breezy was sitting by herself on the edge of the field, stretching. The rest of the team — including Terry — was in the middle of the field warming up.

Peter sat down next to her on the grass. "What's going on?" he wanted to know.

Breezy looked up warily. If Peter started making fun of her television interview, she didn't know what she was going to do. She didn't think he would, though. He was smiling at her. Then again, she didn't think her friends would turn on her either.

"Not too much," Breezy answered. "How are you?"

"Good," he replied. "So, I saw your interview on Sunday."

Here it comes, thought Breezy. Now he's going to tell me what a bingo-head I am and then he's going to say he had no idea I was so conceited.

"You know . . ." Peter began and then looked down

at the grass in front of him. Breezy noticed that his neck was turning bright red.

She might as well get this over with, Breezy figured. Peter was obviously embarrassed for her and didn't know how to say it.

"What?" Breezy asked brusquely.

"I . . . uh . . . I just wanted to say that you looked really good on television," he answered in a rush, still not looking up. "You looked . . . uh . . . glamorous."

Breezy giggled. She had been called a lot of things in the past, but never glamorous. "Yeah, well, I'll be jetting off to Hollywood any day now," she joked.

Peter laughed. "Right," he agreed. "And a pink limo will pick you up from the airport."

Suddenly, Breezy realized that since the interview had aired she hadn't really laughed. Now she was crying she was laughing so hard. Leave it to Peter.

"But seriously," Peter continued, not joking anymore. "I like you the way you are now a lot better than with all that makeup and stuff. You didn't look like the Breezy I know."

Breezy looked down at her blue sweats cut off above the knees, her University of Maryland T-shirt that had definitely seen better days, and the stripes on her socks that didn't match each other. Then she thought of sitting under the hot lights in the studio, feeling as if her hair was shellacked and her face was melting off because of all the makeup. "Me, too," she agreed softly.

They stretched on the grass for a few moments in silence. Breezy wasn't going to bring up the interview again, since Peter didn't seem at all bothered by the way she had appeared. But she needed to talk to someone about it — and none of her friends would listen.

"Do you think I sold out?" Breezy asked Peter quickly before she could change her mind.

"Sold out?" Peter questioned, sounding confused. "What do you mean?"

"Well, we started the Parrots because we were sick of being treated as girls instead of baseball players," Breezy explained. "And I hate it when they write in the papers that I'm a 'girl pitcher.' Why can't they just say I'm a pitcher?"

Peter was silent for a minute. "I never thought of that," he finally admitted. "I guess it does make you sound a little less of a pitcher when they call you a 'girl pitcher.'"

"Right," Breezy agreed. "So then I go and do this television interview and I come off as this total priss who only thinks about herself and boys — worse than Lindsay Cunningham, even."

"I don't think so," Peter protested.

"Well, I do," Breezy replied. "And so does the rest of my team. They aren't talking to me. They think I sold out and I should have boycotted the whole interview. But I was so excited that Melvin Myers actually asked me to be on his show."

"What's he like anyway?" Peter asked, sounding curious.

"He wears a toupee!" Breezy exclaimed, happy that she could finally share that strange fact with someone besides her family.

"No way!" Peter said. "I can't believe it. I mean, he looks like such a dude on television. And he knows all those big stars."

"I know," Breezy agreed. "He also wears a ton of makeup."

"Makeup!?" Peter gasped. "Oh my gosh! I don't think I can ever watch that show again! Melvin Myers wears makeup?"

"And he kept calling me 'little lady' and 'honey' and stuff like that," Breezy admitted, beginning to get angry all over again.

Peter whistled. "You must have given him a really hard time, huh?" he asked. "I can't imagine that you would ever let someone get away with that."

Breezy groaned. "That's just it, Peter," she said, not meeting his eyes. "I did. I let him get away with it. I didn't say anything. I can't believe it."

Peter was quiet as he stretched his hamstrings. "Well, Breezy," he said reasonably, "he *is* Melvin Myers after all. I suppose I would let that dude call me anything if he asked me to be on his show — even if he *does* wear makeup."

"Really?" Breezy asked in disbelief. She suspected

that Peter was saying that just to make her feel better.

"Really," he replied firmly. "Besides, you were on national television, Breeze! I would love to be on the seven o'clock news! Come on, you threw a no-hitter and Melvin Myers called you up and asked you to be on his show. How could you possibly turn that down?"

"I couldn't," Breezy answered.

"And how could you possibly know that he was going to put makeup on you and call you a 'little lady?'" Peter asked logically. "So don't sweat it. I'm sure your teammates would understand if you explained it to them. Have you tried?"

"Well, I did try," Breezy answered. "But the worst part of that whole television thing was that Melvin Myers edited out everything I said about the Parrots. Now they think I've got a huge ego and I don't care about them. I know I couldn't have thrown a no-hitter without them. Why don't they know I know?"

"They'll come around," Peter said positively. "Don't worry about it. Hey, Coach Chang is calling us. We better get over there."

Breezy stood up and reluctantly followed Peter over to the dugout. Even though what he said made sense, she still didn't see how she was going to make the Parrots understand. And since they weren't even talking to her, she didn't think she could explain it to them. If only she could ask Peter to talk to them. But this was something she had to do herself.

"Congratulations once again," Coach Chang said as soon as the All-Stars had gathered in the dugout. "You should all feel very proud that you were chosen for this team. Since you come from different teams and probably don't all know each other, perhaps you should start by introducing yourselves, your team, and the position you play."

Breezy looked around at all the other baseball players. There were only a few players that she did know: Peter, Bobby "Iceman" Brennan, Hector Martinez, Jimmy Hsu, and Terry. It was only just starting to sink in what an incredible honor it was to be chosen for the All-Star team.

"I'll start. I'm Coach Chang and I'm from College Park. I coach the CP Subway Shop team."

Everyone went around introducing themselves. Breezy tried to pay attention, but she was trying to meet Terry's eyes. The Parrots catcher was standing as far away from Breezy as possible without leaving the dugout. Terry had her eyes fixed firmly on the coach, though.

Finally, it was Breezy's turn. "Breezy Hawk," she said shortly. "Pitcher." She paused for a long moment. "Oh, and I play for the Pink Parrots."

"Figures she would almost forget what team she plays for," Terry said to Iceman — loudly.

"Okay, team," Coach Chang announced when everyone was finished. "I have everyone's stats, but I really want to get a sense of how you all play. So, since we've got over 18 players, I think we should have a scrimmage.

Just so I can get a feel for the team and put names with faces."

Then he read off the people on each side. Breezy and Peter were on Team A — but so was Terry. Breezy watched as Terry went over to talk to Coach Chang. Since Team A was in the field first, Breezy just went out into the field. She didn't want to spy on Terry or anything.

Stepping on the mound, Breezy started swinging her arms around to loosen them up. She faced the outfield and twisted from the waist, too. Her muscles felt a little tight, and Breezy hoped she wouldn't pull anything in her arm.

Deciding to take it easy for a little while, Breezy spun around to face Terry behind home plate. Only it wasn't Terry. It was Hector Martinez, the other catcher. Breezy shot a glance at the dugout and saw Terry swinging a bat around. Obviously, she had talked Coach Chang into switching her to Team B.

Breezy gritted her teeth in determination. Fine, she thought angrily. If that's the way she wants it, that's the way she's going to get it. All thoughts of taking it easy went right out the window. Breezy hoped Terry would come up to bat in the first inning. She couldn't wait to face her at the plate. Terry was going to see firsthand why Melvin Myers had wanted to interview Breezy. And it wasn't going to be pretty.

7

"Oh my gosh!" Jazz exclaimed right before the start of the Parrots' game against Dew Drop Inn. Ro had just finished her get-psyched speech and the Parrots were about to take the field. "The stands are packed! I've never seen so many people at one of our games before. Why are there so many here today?"

"Probably to see our big star, with the very big head, Breezy Hawk!" Terry retorted, strapping on her catcher's equipment.

Breezy's dark eyes flashed. Terry had definitely meant for her to hear that. Could Breezy help it that all these people wanted to watch her pitch? Why was Terry so jealous about it, she wondered. Just like that television thing wasn't her fault, neither was this. And now with all these people and reporters here, Breezy was starting to feel pressure to deliver some incredible pitching. It would be hard enough to pitch another three innings of no-hit baseball, but now Breezy also had a problem catcher. For the first time, Breezy wished they had a back-up catcher. Terry just had too much attitude lately.

Tightening the rubber band in her dark blonde pony-tail, Breezy glared at Terry. Then she jammed her baseball cap onto her head and picked up her glove.

"It's a wonder her head can still fit in that hat," Betsy muttered as Breezy walked out of the dugout.

Great, Breezy thought in disgust. She couldn't even count the hours she had put in with Betsy after practice trying to help her become a more consistent batter. And as soon as it *appeared* that Breezy didn't really care about the Parrots, Betsy turned against her. Some payback.

"Let's go, Parrots!" Breezy yelled angrily. It was just like them to hang around in the dugout. The game was starting in a few minutes and they hadn't even warmed up yet. Breezy muttered to herself all the way to the pitcher's mound. "Get a move on!" she screamed when she stepped on the pitching rubber.

"Hey, Breeze," Kim said as she passed by. "Chill out. Everyone else wants to win this game, too."

Sure they did, Breezy thought. They probably all wanted to lose just to make her look bad. No, that wasn't true. Terry would kill someone for even suggesting that she might throw a game. Breezy knew that Terry gave everything she had to every single baseball game. She was like Breezy that way: she played each game as if it were her last. And Kim would be really upset if she knew Breezy thought everyone wanted to lose. The Parrots meant almost as much to Kim as they did to Breezy.

"Come on, you birds!" Ro called from the dugout. "Get these boys out one-two-three!"

Breezy gritted her teeth in determination and faced home plate. She watched Terry saunter out as if she had all day and then squat behind the plate.

Finally, Breezy thought in frustration, as she threw a few warm-up pitches. Terry kept throwing the ball back to her just a little short, so she had to keep stretching to catch it.

"BREE-ZY! BREE-ZY! BREE-ZY!" the crowd started chanting.

Breezy flushed a little as Sean Dunphy, the leadoff batter for Dew Drop Inn, stepped into the on-deck circle. This was all she needed. The Parrots would probably think that she had paid the crowd to do this, or something. She couldn't stop the people from cheering. And to tell the truth, the chanting wasn't really inspiring — it was annoying.

Turning around on the mound, Breezy stared at her cleats for a long moment. It was pretty obvious that all the Parrots thought she was getting a swelled head. But she wasn't. She really wasn't. It was true that after the first day, Breezy had begun to like all the attention she was getting a little — especially when it all started ticking Lindsay off.

But lately, particularly after that television fiasco, she wished the whole thing would just dry up and blow away. Besides, they were all acting as if she had asked for this attention. She hadn't. She didn't call up the television studio and ask for an interview. Did they really believe she had sent her own photo to *The Hampstead Times* and bribed the principal to talk about her over the loudspeaker?

Squaring her shoulders, Breezy suddenly knew exactly what she had to do — she had to prove to her teammates that she was as good as everyone kept saying. She had to just go out and pitch some great baseball. If she could pitch three perfect innings — no hits, no walks, and no errors — that would be awesome, and better than a no-hitter. Three innings would be a good start. It was half the game, after all.

"Batter up!" the umpire yelled as Sean stepped into the batter's box.

Breezy spun around and faced Terry. The catcher glared at her and called for a fastball. Breezy wound up and delivered a rocket. Zip! Right over the center of the plate.

"Stee-rike one!" the umpire yelled.

Grinning despite herself, Breezy shook out her arm. That was a *fast*ball, she thought. She wondered if that had put a hole in Terry's glove. Then she smiled. Her arm felt great — really loose and really fast. Perfect baseball didn't seem so impossible right then.

Terry held down three fingers and patted her leg once. That was the signal for an outside sidearm fastball.

"BREE-ZY! BREE-ZY! BREE-ZY!" the fans cheered

loudly, suddenly reminding the pitcher of their presence.

Breezy shook her head to make the noise go away and then focused on Terry's mitt. She wound up and shot the ball toward Sean. He shifted his weight and took a big swing. Breezy held her breath until she saw that Sean had swung too high and her pitch had gone under his bat. Breezy sighed in relief. It would have been terrible to blow a perfect three innings on the first batter.

One more, Breezy thought as she faced Terry again. The catcher was still glaring at her. Two great pitches, and Terry's still angry. Breezy realized then that nothing she could do would be right in Terry's eyes. But since pitching was what she knew best, she'd have to go for it anyway.

Terry called for a sinker. Breezy grinned as she watched her pitch drop almost three feet before it reached the plate. No way was Sean going to even get a piece of that. And he didn't. Three pitches. Three strikes. One out.

"Way to go, girl!" Ro called from the dugout. "Keep it up!"

Smiling, Breezy caught the ball back from Terry and turned around, facing the field. She wanted to share this with her teammates. But when she looked around, none of them would so much as glance toward her. Even Kim was totally focused on the batter. Then it struck her that she hadn't heard any infield chatter since the start of the game. Usually everyone was yelling encouragement to each other. At that moment, Breezy suddenly realized how very important that chatter was to her.

Breezy spun around angrily, even more determined to pitch well. Fine, she thought. If they didn't care, she would just have to pitch a game that they *had* to care about.

Andy Gable, Dew Drop Inn's third baseman, stared at her from home plate. "You won't get me that easily!" he called out to Breezy.

Breezy fired a fastball up the inside of the plate. Andy reacted quickly and got his bat around in time. But he only chipped at it and the ball popped up right over his head.

"I got it!" Breezy screamed, running in toward the plate.

"*I* got it!" Terry yelled, jumping up and throwing off her mask.

Breezy stopped short. "Fine," she said, dropping her glove to her side.

"Out!" the umpire called as Terry made the catch easily.

Tossing the ball back to Breezy, Terry narrowed her green eyes. "Pop-ups behind or over the plate are mine," she said shortly. "Please remember that."

Breezy nodded and turned abruptly back toward the mound. The pitcher always covered for the catcher in situations like that, and Terry knew that. Why was she pulling this attitude now? Breezy wondered if it had anything to do with the fact that she had struck Terry out in the All-Star practice.

"Let's go, Breeze!" someone from the stands yelled.

The voice sounded familiar and Breezy searched the bleachers until she spotted her little brother, Danny, sitting with all of his friends. He smiled and waved at her. "Come on, Breezy!" he screamed.

She grinned back at him. It was good to know that she had a little support out there.

"Batter up!" the umpire called out as Chris Barclay swaggered from the on-deck circle to the plate.

Lazily, Chris raised his bat to his shoulder and glanced toward Breezy. She could tell by his attitude that he was not very impressed by her pitching.

Breezy sent her first pitch up the very inside of the plate, brushing Chris back so quickly he stumbled and fell down. That should impress him, she thought, as he dusted off his uniform pants.

But Chris caught a piece of Breezy's second pitch, a change-up. He didn't get a lot of power on his bat and he swung under the ball. The ball went flying in a high, slow arc out to Jazz in rightfield.

"Come on, get under it," Breezy muttered as her cousin ran in toward the ball.

The ball slowly began its descent and Jazz raised her glove to meet it. Breezy almost couldn't bear to watch the action and wanted more than anything to squeeze her eyes shut. But at the same time she wasn't able to tear her eyes away.

Breezy breathed a sigh of relief as the ball dropped into Jazz's glove. "No!" she screamed, as the ball bounced out because Jazz forgot to close her glove around it and trap it with her other hand.

Jazz scrambled on the ground for the ball and finally got it in her hand. She threw the ball toward Crystal, but it fell far short. Crystal ran out to pick it up. By the time the first baseman had it, Chris was already safely on second.

"No problem!" Chris called to his dugout. "I don't know what you guys were so worried about! Piece of cake!"

Breezy groaned. She couldn't believe her cousin had ruined the perfect start to three perfect innings! At least the dropped catch counted as an error, so Breezy could still throw no-hit ball for three innings.

"*Two* hands!" Breezy screamed at Jazz. "You're supposed to use two hands every time you make a catch!"

"Leave her alone!" Terry yelled from the plate. "You just worry about yourself, okay? It was *your* pitch he hit."

What was Terry talking about? Breezy was the captain. She couldn't just worry about herself. It was her job to worry about everybody else on the team.

"There are two outs," Breezy called out, ignoring Terry. "The play is to first base. Let's retire them!"

No one else said anything. Usually, a round of encouraging cheers followed. Instead, the field was deathly quiet. Breezy couldn't get used to it.

"Sam 'The Man!'" Chris yelled as his teammate stepped up to bat. "Bring me home!"

Dew Drop Inn's big centerfielder tapped the dirt off the bottom of his right cleat with his bat and then leisurely stepped into the batter's box. Sam "The Man" Bell was a slugger with incredible power, but Breezy also knew he was pretty inconsistent. She could bring him down swinging if she went about it correctly.

Terry called for a sidearm fastball. Breezy shook off the signal. Sam loved first-pitch fastballs. There was no way she was going to make it easy for Dew Drop Inn. Pitching a fastball to "The Man" was like handing him a home run on a silver platter. Terry should know better. It was the catcher's job to learn all the batters' stats, strengths, and weaknesses.

Glaring at Breezy, Terry ignored her shake off and called for the sidearm fastball again. Breezy shook her head again.

"Time!" Terry called out, stood up, and threw off her mask. She marched out to the pitcher's mound.

Breezy was waiting with her hands on her hips. "What?" she asked shortly as she popped a piece of gum in her mouth.

"Why are you shaking off my signs?" Terry asked, her eyes narrowing.

"You shouldn't be calling for a fastball on the first pitch to Bell," Breezy retorted, blowing a big bubble. "Get with the program, Terry."

"Fine," Terry said, practically biting off the word. "You want to call your own pitches, too? Go right ahead. Let's see how you do."

Terry spun around and stalked back to home plate without even waiting for Breezy to reply.

Shaking her head in disgust, Breezy studied the back of her catcher. She couldn't call her own pitches. Then she'd have to think too much. Breezy knew all too well that pitchers shouldn't think, they should just throw.

Breezy counted on Terry. Sure, Breezy knew some of the batters and their strengths — like Sam's — but she couldn't really concentrate on that when she was pitching. It was too distracting. Breezy knew she couldn't have thrown the no-hitter without Terry. It was Terry's no-hitter as much as it was Breezy's.

This game was turning into a battlefield, Breezy thought, kicking the dirt. She didn't know what to do. She couldn't very well just march up to Terry and apologize. Breezy didn't think she had done anything wrong. What would she apologize for? Breezy thought Terry should be the one doing the apologizing.

"Just pitch," Breezy muttered to herself as she faced Terry. The catcher didn't move a muscle. She obviously meant what she had said — Breezy could call her own pitches.

She should throw a sinker, Breezy thought, rubbing the ball with her right hand. But if Sam got under the ball, it would be gone. And she couldn't throw the fastball. He would kill it. That left the change-up. But would Sam be expecting that pitch, since he knew she wouldn't throw a fastball?

Breezy shook her head, trying to clear it. She wondered if Terry went through all this indecision on every pitch. How did the catcher do it? Breezy set her jaw and decided to go for the change-up. Otherwise, she'd be standing there all day trying to figure out what to pitch.

Winding up and delivering, Breezy held her breath until the ball hit Terry's glove.

"Stee-rike one!" the umpire called.

Sam stepped out of the batter's box and readjusted his batting helmet. He pulled on his batting glove and tucked his uniform shirt in again.

Breezy waited patiently, her right foot on the pitching rubber. If nothing else, Sam's delay (he liked playing mind games) would give her time to decide what to throw next.

Finally, Sam crouched back in his batting stance. He swung his bat a few times as he stared at Breezy. A fastball, Breezy decided. Maybe she could catch him off balance, since most pitchers wouldn't dare throw him something straight up the plate.

Breezy's pitch never hit Terry's mitt. Sam's bat was a

blur as he brought it around. *Thwack*! The bat and the ball made solid contact. The ball shot out straight in a line drive right up the third baseline.

Andrea, playing the "Hot Corner," as third base is also called, took three quick steps to the right and then dove. She snagged the ball before it hit the dirt.

Breezy grinned, not believing it. She had worked with Andrea a lot on making just that play. Andrea had always complained about diving, and never, ever did it in practice. She moaned about the dust and getting dirty. And here she made a major clutch play in a big game and ended up in the dirt. At least something had paid off, Breezy thought happily.

"Way to go!" Breezy yelled as she trotted in toward the dugout. She was batting first, and she wanted to get in a few practice swings before she was up.

Grabbing her helmet and her bat, Breezy started out to the on-deck circle. Making sure to walk by Andrea before leaving the dugout, Breezy patted her on the back. "Great catch, Andrea!" she congratulated the third baseman. "I knew you could do it!"

Andrea glanced toward Breezy, a startled expression on her face. "Uh . . . thanks . . . Breezy," she said hesitantly. Then she smiled. "I guess all that hard work paid off, right?"

Breezy nodded, not understanding why Andrea looked so surprised at her praise. Breezy always congratulated a Parrot after a good play, especially a great one like Andrea's. "Definitely," she agreed, walking out of the dugout and heading over to the on-deck circle.

"She actually noticed someone else's play?" someone asked snidely as Breezy left the dugout.

Blinking furiously, Breezy jammed her helmet on her head. She couldn't even say one little thing without getting some abuse. This whole situation was getting totally out of hand, and Breezy didn't know how to get it back under control.

As she swung the bat, Breezy suddenly decided she would talk to Kim after the game. They were best friends, after all. Breezy knew that if she explained the whole television thing to Kim, she would understand. And maybe she would know what to do about the rest of the Parrots.

"Batter up!" the umpire screamed, breaking into Breezy's thoughts.

Taking a deep breath, Breezy stepped up to the plate and faced Sean Dunphy, Dew Drop Inn's pitcher. She knew she had to get a hit. She couldn't walk back into that dugout.

Sean's first pitch was way too low, and Breezy took it for ball one. His next pitch screamed up the middle of the plate. Breezy swung hard and connected solidly, but she didn't follow through on her swing and the ball flew into the stands for a foul. Strike one.

Now the count was one and one. Breezy gripped her bat and glared at Sean. He must have been a little rattled by her quick contact with the ball, and threw two balls in a row. He worked the count full by getting Breezy to take a mighty swing at a sneaky change-up.

"Come on, Breeze!" Ro screamed. "Keep your eye on the ball. Get something going here!"

Breezy choked up a little on the bat and crouched a bit lower. Putting all her weight on her back leg, Breezy stared at Sean, daring him to throw a strike at her.

Breezy grinned and jumped back from the plate as the ball whizzed by. She wasn't able to tell if the ball was too far inside or not, but she jumped back as if it was going to hit her anyway. Sometimes, if the pitch was close and the batter jumped back, the umpire would automatically call it a ball. Maybe because he thought that the batter knew something he didn't. It would be even better if she dropped her bat and started toward first base as if there was no question that it was a ball. Whatever it was, Breezy did whatever she could to get on base. And if it meant drawing a walk, that was cool.

"Ball four!" the umpire yelled as Breezy flung her bat and trotted toward first. "Take your base."

Standing on first base, Breezy took off her batting glove and stuck it in her back pocket. "Keep us alive!" Breezy yelled at Crystal who was up next.

Sean was a little rattled by the walk and sent a slow fastball to Crystal — right down the middle of the plate. She blooped it out to the hole between the second baseman and the centerfielder.

Breezy took off for second, sliding as she saw the ball coming toward the bag. Getting up and dusting herself off, Breezy didn't even have to hear the umpire's call to know that she was safe. She beat the throw by a mile.

"All right!" Breezy cheered, clapping her hands. "Let's go, Kim!"

Kim bunted up the first baseline. It was a beautiful sacrifice play because even though she got snagged at first, Breezy and Crystal advanced a base.

"Come on!" Breezy yelled to Terry who always batted fourth, the cleanup position. "We're both in scoring position! Bring us home!"

Breezy didn't think it was strange to be cheering for Terry, even though they weren't getting along. Breezy knew it shouldn't make a difference once they got out on the field. They were on the same team, and anything else could wait until after the game was over and the Parrots had won. Breezy was mad at herself for losing her cool when she was pitching. She should have just let Terry keep calling the pitches.

On Sean's third pitch, with the count one and one, Terry sent a mammoth shot out to rightfield. The ball hit the dirt in the warning track. The rightfielder played the ball off the wall and rifled it to his first baseman who then shot it toward home. It was too late, though. Breezy and Crystal had already scored. The Parrots were up 2-0.

Finally, the dugout started to come alive. "Way to go, Ter!" Kim shouted.

"What a shot!" Betsy added.

"All right, girl!" Ro yelled from the dugout.

Sean suddenly found a groove and struck out both Sarah and Jazz. But Breezy wasn't that upset — even though Jazz swung at some obvious balls. The Parrots had jumped to an early lead and they were starting to gain some momentum.

As Breezy trotted out to the pitcher's mound, she smiled as she suddenly heard the sound of some infield chatter. It was good to have her team back.

Neither the Parrots nor Dew Drop Inn could get anything going in the second inning, and the third started as the first had ended, with the Parrots up by two.

Breezy struck out the first Dew Drop Inn batter and then faced the second, Andy Gable. Andy was a small, wiry, blond-haired boy who played third base. He stepped into the batter's box and took a few short swings.

Breezy started to go through her inner debate about what pitch to throw. She couldn't believe how difficult it was. As she listened to the chatter behind her, Breezy knew she had been right. She only had to pitch a good game and the team would rally. And she was almost done with her stint. If she could just get through this inning, she would have a half-game of no-hit ball. Not a bad follow-up to her last game.

Looking around at her teammates, Breezy noticed Jazz doing handstands out in rightfield. "That girl," Breezy muttered. "Pay attention, Jazz!" she yelled.

"Stop picking on her!" Terry screamed.

Suddenly, Breezy was angry again. Picking on her? Breezy knew she wasn't picking on Jazz; she just wanted her to pay attention. What if Andy hit the ball out there and Jazz was in the middle of a handstand? Breezy wondered why Terry was all over her like that. It was crazy.

Staring at her catcher, Breezy's anger started welling up, threatening to spill over. She wasn't even thinking about Andy Gable, the batter, and what kind of pitch she ought to throw to him. All Breezy wanted at that moment was to throw a supersonic fastball and calm down a little.

She wound up and put everything she had into the ball. It rocketed toward Terry, near the inside of the plate.

It happened so quickly, Breezy wasn't sure how. The ball was too far inside, and it rose a bit. The pitch was headed right for Andy, but he didn't realize that until it was too late. He tried to duck, but wasn't fast enough. Breezy's supersonic fastball hit him square in the head and Andy went down — hard.

Breezy stood on the pitcher's mound with her mouth open. She had never hit a batter before. Staring at Andy lying on the ground, Breezy suddenly realized that he wasn't moving.

8

"He's out cold!" Coach O'Toole, Dew Drop Inn's coach, called out. "Don't move him! Get a doctor!"

Breezy hadn't moved since she had hit Andy.

"It wasn't your fault, Breeze," Kim said, suddenly coming up behind her.

"Huh?" Breezy asked, tilting her head toward Kim. She hadn't really heard what Kim had said. She could only see Andy, lying there in the dirt.

Finally, Andy moved. He sat up and looked around the field, with a totally dazed expression on his face. Coach O'Toole helped him to his feet. Andy looked very wobbly as they walked to the Dew Drop Inn dugout.

"Okay, people!" the umpire called out. "Excitement's over! Can we have a pinch runner on first?"

Ross Benson trotted over to first base.

"Smooth move," he said to Breezy as he ran by.

"Batter up!" the umpire yelled.

Kim rubbed Breezy's back. "Don't sweat it, Breeze," Kim said. "Just put it out of your mind." Then Kim turned and walked back to her position at shortstop.

Breezy shook her head to clear it. Kim's words finally started to sink in. Breezy looked around for the ball and realized that she didn't have it. Glancing up, she saw Terry walking toward her.

"How's it going, Breezy?" Terry asked, handing her the ball. Nodding, Breezy slapped the ball into her glove.

"Listen, I'll start calling the pitches again," Terry added, as she turned back to the plate. "Don't think, okay? Just throw."

Breezy nodded again, barely realizing that Terry was being like her old self again. Pulling her hat lower on her head, Breezy faced Terry.

Holding down one finger, Terry called for a fastball. Breezy took a deep breath, wound up, and delivered the pitch. Afraid to hit Chris, Breezy aimed away from him. The ball went about two feet wide of the plate.

Terry scrambled for the ball and shot it back to Breezy. The pitcher took another deep breath and kicked the dirt with her foot. Every time she looked at Chris, she saw Andy lying in the dirt. Even though Chris was not crowding the plate at all, Breezy didn't want to take the chance. She was going to throw outside.

And she did. Her next three pitches were way outside. Four straight balls. Breezy didn't think she had ever thrown four straight balls in her life.

Terry took another walk out to the mound. "Hey, Breeze," she said. "How are you doing?"

"Fine," Breezy replied, taking off her hat and tightening her ponytail. She jammed her hat back on her head.

"Listen, Breeze," Terry went on as if she hadn't heard Breezy. "You're not getting anything at all on your fastball. You've got to get your body into it."

Breezy didn't say anything. She couldn't tell Terry that she was afraid of throwing hard.

Suddenly, a siren wailed closer and closer. Breezy looked around and saw an ambulance pull up onto the field and stop behind Dew Drop Inn's dugout.

Breezy dropped the ball on the ground without even realizing that it had left her hand. The only thing she saw was the stretcher that was being pulled from the dugout to the ambulance. Andy Gable was lying on it, looking very white and frail. He was covered with blankets and strapped on the stretcher.

Breezy didn't move until the ambulance wailed away. *She* was responsible for that. What if Andy was really hurt, Breezy wondered. What if he died? Breezy remembered reading something about a Yankee pitcher, Carl Mays was his name, who hit a guy named Ray Chapman in the head with a pitch. Chapman had died the next day. She shuddered.

"Breeze!" Terry said loudly. "Are you still with us?"

"Huh?" Breezy asked, feeling very disoriented.

"You dropped the ball," Terry pointed out. "Come on, just finish up the inning. You can do it."

Breezy shook her head. "I can't," she said softly. "I

can't do it." Then she turned and walked toward the Parrots' dugout.

"Breeze!" Terry called out, but Breezy didn't even turn around.

Breezy sat down in the dugout and faced the field, feeling kind of shell-shocked. She had put a kid in the hospital! Remembering a story about how Iceman had done the same thing the year before, Breezy didn't know how he had kept pitching. She was too afraid of hitting someone else.

"Okay, Sarah!" Ro yelled. "Get in there and pitch!"

Sarah Fishman trotted in from centerfield to the pitcher's mound.

"Jamie!" Ro called, looking around the dugout. Jamie Liu, the newest Parrot, stood up. "Go play center!"

Jamie grabbed her glove and ran out onto the field, her black braid streaming out behind her.

"How are you doing, hon?" Ro asked, sitting down next to Breezy. "I know I would be pretty shaken up."

Breezy nodded her head miserably.

"Don't worry about it, Breezy," Ro said, putting her arm around her.

They watched Sarah take her warm-up pitches for a few minutes. If Breezy started, Sarah didn't usually pitch until the fourth inning. She was obviously not prepared to pitch so soon — it was only the third inning. Her pitches were all over the place.

"Batter up!" the umpire yelled.

Ro glanced over at Breezy with a worried look on her face. "I've got to keep stats," Ro said, apologizing to Breezy. "Are you going to be all right? You don't have to stay if you don't want to. You can just go home."

"I'm the captain," Breezy answered. "I can't leave."

Wincing every time Sarah pitched inside, Breezy forced herself to watch. She knew that in all probability Sarah wouldn't hit Sam "The Man," but Breezy kept seeing him lying on the dirt in her mind. She blinked, trying to clear her head.

Then Terry called for a fastball. Sarah delivered it right over the plate. Sam gave a mighty swing and sent the ball flying out to centerfield. Breezy held her breath as Jamie tried to get in position under the ball. But the ball kept rising.

"It's out of here!" Sam yelled, as he chucked his bat and trotted toward first.

Breezy couldn't help herself; she whistled in admiration. That was a towering home run. She sighed, though, as she realized that the score was now tied at 2-2.

Sarah buckled down and made Robert Collins pop up to Kim for the second out. Then she struck out Mike Dickerson to end the inning.

Sighing in relief, Breezy watched her teammates straggle into the dugout. She tried to think of something to say that would get them moving again, but absolutely nothing came to mind. What could *she* say? She had put another player in the hospital.

Kim came in and sat down next to Breezy. "How's it going, Breeze?" she asked, swinging her short legs on the bench. "Don't worry about it. I'm sure Andy will be okay. He wasn't unconscious anymore or anything."

Flashing back to Andy's ghost-white face as they wheeled him to the ambulance, Breezy didn't really feel better. What if he had internal injuries or something? Her fastball might not have killed him, but maybe it had caused some brain damage. One week a pitching star, the next, a murderer. It was too terrible to think about.

The Parrots were up and down, one, two, three. They headed back to the field, still tied with Dew Drop Inn. Breezy suddenly realized that the Parrots were going to be in a real bind in the sixth inning. Since Breezy had taken herself out in the third inning, Sarah had to pitch the rest of that inning. Unfortunately, even though she had only pitched part of the inning, it counted as a whole inning for Sarah. She could only pitch two more innings. And because Breezy had already pitched and come out, she couldn't go back in the game as a pitcher. So the Parrots were going to have to put someone else on the mound in the sixth. Breezy had no idea who. Kim had pitched before when Breezy had been hurt last month, but Breezy knew she hated it. Who else was left?

Sarah struggled again in the fourth, and Dew Drop Inn got three more runs before the side was retired. Once again, the Parrots failed to get anything going in their at-bat and began the fifth inning down by three.

Breezy knew, as captain, that she should be rallying her team, but for the first time, she didn't know how. Sarah gave up two more runs in the fifth and Dew Drop Inn was now winning 7-2. It was getting ugly.

Terry led off in the bottom of the fifth and tried to get something going. She smacked a line-drive double out to deep centerfield. But she tried to stretch her double into a triple and got snagged at third base. One out.

Sarah got on base safely, but then Jazz struck out. Julie popped up to the third baseman. He misjudged it, though, and he was positioned too far forward when the ball finally dropped.

The Parrots had runners on first and second and Andrea drew a walk. Now the bases were loaded. Breezy started to feel a little hopeful. If only the Parrots could come back, maybe she wouldn't feel so bad.

Then Betsy hit a pop-up foul ball that the first baseman was able to get under and the Parrots were retired, with three birds stranded on base.

The sixth inning was a disaster. No one wanted to pitch. Kim tried first, but only lasted a batter and a half before pulling herself out. Then Crystal gave it a try, but she didn't have a windup at all so there was no power on any of her pitches. It was torture to watch, and Breezy was thankful that Dew Drop Inn only got four runs out of it. It could have been a lot worse.

In the bottom of the sixth, the Parrots were again out one, two, three. Breezy couldn't even bear to watch. She pulled her cap over her eyes and tried not to think about Andy Gable. The Parrots lost the game 11-2.

"Great," Terry said sarcastically, as she threw her batting helmet into the pile of bats at the end of the game. They all clattered loudly onto the cement floor of the dugout. "They slaughtered us."

Breezy could tell that the team was really down.

"Come on, girls!" Ro said, trying to cheer everyone up. "You gave it your best shot. It's hard to come back from something like what happened in the third inning. At least you didn't give up."

"Right," Terry continued. "Like our pitcher did?"

"What do you mean by that?" Breezy asked, her dark eyes blazing. She stood up and squared off with Terry.

"It's pretty obvious, Breezy," Terry retorted. "You didn't even try out there after you hit Andy. You just quit. Up and left the team. I didn't even hear any cheering from the dugout with you sitting here. Some captain you are. And I thought you were this incredible pitcher. You're so great you've even been on television. What's with you now? You couldn't take a little pressure?"

"Hey, Breeze," Kim cut in quickly. "Don't pay attention to her. I know it must have been hard to put Andy and the ambulance and all out of your mind."

"You think I was worried about him?" Breezy asked, grabbing her glove. "Think again. It wasn't *my* fault. He just didn't duck fast enough, okay? That wasn't the problem. I was worried about my catcher."

"What?" Kim asked, sounding shocked.

"Yeah," Breezy continued. "She's got this major attitude and wasn't even doing her job. She actually stopped calling the pitches and made me do it. Real responsible, huh? Really sounds like she wanted the team to win, right?"

"You think I didn't want the team to win?" Terry retorted, taking a step toward Breezy. "Is that what you think? Well, we already know how much loyalty you've got to this team. We all saw it on national television."

Suddenly, Breezy had had it. No one ever gave her the benefit of the doubt. That plus hitting Andy just added up to too much. "Sure you saw it!" Breezy exploded. "But did you ever think what you saw wasn't all I said? Do you really think that I could throw a no-hitter without the rest of the team? Great to know that you all trust me so much! I'm really glad that I found out now that all my supposed friends were behind me all the way. You never even asked me about my side of the story!"

Breezy glared at all the Parrots. Even Ro stared back at her with a surprised look on her face. No one said anything for a moment.

"Well, since you all obviously think I just gave up out there and threw the game away and that the Parrots don't mean anything to me anyway, I'll make it easy on you," Breezy continued. "I quit!"

Then before anyone could react, Breezy stormed out of the dugout without a backward glance.

9

"Don't slam the door!" Mrs. Hawk yelled just as Breezy slammed the door behind her.

Striding down the front walk, Breezy jammed her hands in the pockets of her jeans. She couldn't stay inside for one more minute — she was way too wound up. The All-Star Game was the next morning, and Breezy had no idea how she was going to pitch when she still had Andy Gable on her mind. Even though she had found out that he only had a concussion and he hadn't even had to spend the night in the hospital or anything, she still felt awful. The fact that it could have been a lot worse didn't seem to help much either.

School that day, though, had been the worst. The Parrots had avoided her like she had the plague or something — even Kim. She had been glad to get home.

Playing catch with Russ and Danny in the backyard, Breezy realized how much she missed the Parrots. Even though she had only quit the team the day before, she felt as if some big part of her life was gone.

When Breezy had quit the Mitchell Lumber team, she did not have a second thought about it. She had known that she had done the right thing. Now, she wasn't so sure about quitting the Parrots. It was *her* team after all — she had started it. She and Kim. The more she had thought about it as she tried to eat a little of the spaghetti and meatballs her mother had made, which she usually loved, the more she thought she had to do something about it. She couldn't stand the situation for one more second.

After dinner Breezy decided to head over to Kim's. She had no idea what she was going to say or anything, but she just knew she had to go.

"Hey, Breezy," Kim said, suddenly coming around the corner and stopping in front of Breezy.

"Hi, Kim," Breezy replied, feeling a little off-balance. She was still unsure of what to say to her best friend and she had figured she'd have the rest of the walk to the Yardleys' to think about it. But here was Kim, right in front of her.

"I was just on my way to see you," Kim admitted.

Breezy laughed, feeling better about things than she had in a long time.

"What's so funny?" Kim demanded, throwing one red braid over her shoulder. She put her hands on her hips and glared up at Breezy.

"I was just on my way to see *you*," Breezy said.

Kim started to laugh, too. "Really?"

"Yeah," Breezy confirmed, scuffing the toe of her sneaker on a crack in the sidewalk.

There was a long pause and then both girls started talking at once. "I wanted to tell you I was sorry," Kim and Breezy said at the same time.

They looked at each other and cracked up again. Every time Breezy thought she'd be able to stop laughing, she looked at Kim and she'd start again.

About five minutes later, both girls got under control.

"We should have listened to your side of the story," Kim admitted, wiping tears from her eyes. "You were right. We should have known that you would never forget about us."

"Well, I probably should have told you sooner," Breezy said. "Do you want to come back over to my house?" she asked, changing the subject. "We can make chocolate chip cookies. Besides, the mosquitoes are eating me alive!"

"Cookies!" Kim exclaimed. "Will you let me eat some of the batter this time?"

"As long as there's enough left for cookies," Breezy replied, turning back toward her house.

After the girls got back to the Hawks', they mixed up the batter. It wasn't until the first batch of cookies was in the oven that they started talking about the Parrots again.

"You know," Breezy began, pouring two big glasses of milk, "you guys were totally right about WXRK."

"Why?" Kim asked, eating a spoonful of batter. "Because they did the whole 'girl pitcher' thing?"

"Definitely," Breezy replied and then started laughing. "You're not going to believe this, but Melvin Myers wears a toupee!"

"No way!" Kim exclaimed, squealing. "A toupee!"

"He actually gets it glued on before he goes on the air," Breezy said, opening the oven to check the cookies.

"Glued on?" Kim asked. "With real glue?"

"Yeah, this dude Victor, the makeup guy, brushed glue on the bald part of his head and then patted the toupee down on top of it," Breezy answered. "And Melvin wears a ton of makeup."

"Makeup?" Kim asked in disbelief. "Seriously?"

"Really," Breezy confirmed. "I have, like, no respect for the guy anymore. I wonder what all those sports stars really think of him."

"Maybe they just act nice to him because they want to be on his show," Kim guessed.

"I bet you're right," Breezy said. "You know, the guy even wanted me to wear a dress on television! All that other stuff they did to me was bad enough!"

"A dress!" Kim said loudly, giggling. "Breeze, you don't even *own* a dress!"

The timer suddenly buzzed and Breezy pulled the tray of cookies out of the oven. Kim scooped them onto a plate. Both girls couldn't wait for them to cool, and started eating them right away.

"Mmm!" Breezy mumbled, her mouth full. "These are

great. I love chocolate chip cookies when they're warm!"

"Me too," Kim agreed. "You know, you didn't look that bad on television. In fact, you looked really good. You just didn't look like yourself."

"Really," Breezy said firmly. "I didn't even recognize myself in the mirror when Victor was finished with me."

"So, besides wearing fake hair and makeup, what was Melvin Myers like?" Kim asked, sounding curious.

"He kept calling me 'little lady' and 'hon' and stuff like that," Breezy said, her nose wrinkling in distaste as she thought about it.

"Oh, you must have loved that!" Kim said, laughing. "I can just picture it. You probably gave him what for."

"That's what Peter said, too," Breezy admitted, suddenly serious. She turned to Kim. "But you know something? I didn't. I just let him call me that. Just like I let him do all that stuff to my hair and ask me questions about boys. Kim, you guys were so right about it. I should have listened to you and boycotted the show."

Kim took a long sip of milk. "Breezy, I wouldn't have passed up a chance to be on national television and I don't think any of the other Parrots would have either."

"But you wouldn't have let them put all that makeup on you," Breezy said. "And I *know* Terry wouldn't."

"Breeze, remember who you're talking to here," Kim replied, snitching another spoonful of batter. "You know I let my mother talk me into wearing white patent leather shoes, a white hat, and white *gloves* every Easter."

Breezy giggled. "That's pretty bad," she said.

"And you can't be so sure about Terry either," Kim added. "You know she went over to Ro's with Jazz and got made over that time for the Spring Fling dance."

"That's true," Breezy said, nodding. "I guess you're right. But I still feel pretty bad about it."

"Well, don't," Kim replied matter-of-factly. "So are you ready for the All-Star Game tomorrow?"

"I guess," Breezy answered. Andy Gable was still in the back her mind. But she didn't know how to tell Kim that. Kim might think she was wussing out again. Breezy really didn't know if she could pitch the next day.

"Wemble is incredible," Kim said, not commenting on Breezy's indecisiveness. "They've won the last ten years straight. We've got to win this year."

"I guess," Breezy repeated.

"Aren't you excited about it?" Kim asked. "I mean, we weren't even playing in the Emblem games last year, and now you're on the All-Star team!"

"I guess," Breezy said yet again. Then she grinned. "I'll tell you, Kim, I'm more excited that the Pink Parrots are still ahead of Mitchell Lumber in the standings — even after our loss. We should make it to the playoffs this year, no problem!"

"We?" Kim asked, smiling at her friend. "Does that mean that you're not quitting after all?"

"Quit?" Breezy asked in shock. "I couldn't quit the Parrots. It would be like cutting off my arm."

"Really," Kim agreed. "I can see the headlines: GIRL PITCHER MYSTERIOUSLY LOSES ARM."

Breezy threw a pot holder at Kim. "Really funny, Kim," she giggled. "Really funny."

After Kim had gone home, Breezy went outside. The summer before, her father had painted a square on the side of the garage for her because Breezy had been worried about her consistency. So Breezy used the square to work on control, aiming at it with a tennis ball.

Thunk. Thunk. Thunk. Breezy threw the ball at the garage, grabbed the ball, and threw it back quickly without thinking about what she was throwing.

Breezy thought about Kim asking her if she was excited about the All-Star Game. She had been so excited a week ago, when she had found out she had made the team. Now she just couldn't wait for the whole thing to be over. She felt as if so much stuff had happened since then. She just didn't know if she could pitch anymore.

That afternoon, Breezy had overheard Joey Carpenter saying that he should have been on the All-Star team and that the coaches had made a mistake choosing a girl pitcher — a girl who had tried to kill another player.

Clenching the tennis ball in her hand, Breezy knew she had to pitch. She was representing Emblem, and the Parrots, and she couldn't let them down. Everyone was counting on her. And because she had thrown that no-hitter the week before, they were all expecting great things from her. Breezy just hoped she could deliver.

10

"Snap!" Breezy said to herself, as she walked onto the field the next morning. *This* was what a major league stadium looked like. It was huge! Breezy felt as if she was in a cathedral or something. She walked over to the perfectly raked pitcher's mound. They had moved all the bases in, as well as the pitcher's mound, for this game. Major leaguers pitched from 60 feet away from home plate. Breezy threw from 46 feet out.

Putting one foot on the rubber, Breezy barely heard the sighs and exclamations of her teammates. She turned around and around, looking at the almost empty stands. She had been to see a lot of Orioles games before, but the stadium hadn't appeared to be nearly this big from the stands.

The game didn't start for an hour, so very few fans were at the stadium. The Emblem team had gotten there early to warm up. Breezy had a suspicion that Coach Chang had wanted them to get used to the size of the stadium, too. It was so incredibly huge.

Breezy looked out into the outfield, where some of her teammates were running around. Luckily, they had put up some temporary outfield fences just for the day. She couldn't imagine anyone in Emblem hitting a 400-foot home run — not even Peter or Terry.

They had heard a rumor, though, about this guy, Duane Robinson, who played on the Wemble team. Supposedly he had hit a 400-foot home run the week before. Someone also said that major league scouts were already talking to Duane — he was that good.

Shaking her head, Breezy spun around and looked over at home plate. She took a deep breath. Terry was walking toward her.

"I told Chang he had to play you when he played me," Breezy announced, prepared for a fight. "I'm in relief today — last three innings. And so are you." She didn't know if Terry had talked to Kim the night before or anything. Breezy had been late for the bus that morning. By the time she had finally hopped on, Terry was already sitting with Iceman and the only empty seat was the front seat — next to Coach Chang. So Breezy hadn't had a chance to talk to Terry yet.

"I told him that we pitched a great no-hitter last week," Breezy went on quickly, not giving Terry a chance to answer. "And I said that if he wanted me to help Emblem maintain any kind of lead, I couldn't do it without you."

Breezy stared at Terry as if she was daring her catcher

to say something in protest about the arrangement.

"Okay," Terry said, grinning. "Sounds cool to me. Same signals as usual?"

"Cool," Breezy replied, smiling back at her catcher. "Let's give Wemble something to remember."

Terry cracked her gum and turned and walked back to home plate. "This joint is huge!" she called to Breezy over her shoulder.

Breezy nodded even though she knew Terry couldn't see her. The size of the stadium had almost left her speechless. She was glad she had Terry back on her side. Now she had to make sure she was completely focused on the game — and Andy Gable was out of her mind.

"Hey, Breeze!" Iceman called out as he trotted out to the mound. "Are we going to rock and roll all over Wemble today, or what?"

Laughing, Breezy nodded. If anyone could get Emblem off to a good start, it was Iceman. With his black wraparound sunglasses; short, spiked black hair that was long in the back; big, muscular build; and black glove, Iceman was an imposing presence on the mound. And he had a wicked fastball.

"Hec and I are going to warm up now," Iceman stated, nodding at his catcher, Hector Martinez. "I need the mound."

"No prob," Breezy replied, slapping Iceman's glove with her own. "Just do it!"

"You got it!" Iceman answered, already focusing his

attention on home plate and the approaching game.

Breezy turned around and jogged to the outfield. She wanted to get a little running in before she had to sit in the dugout. Breezy hoped she didn't have any problem sitting out the first three innings. Since there weren't a lot of players on the Parrots, everyone almost always played the whole game. Because there were so many people on the All-Star team, the entire lineup would be changed to give everyone a chance to play. Breezy would only play the last three innings. She wasn't used to sitting around, watching the action. She had had enough of that at the Parrots' last game.

After she had run around the outfield a few times, Breezy started stretching. Her muscles felt warm and loose.

"How's it going?" Jimmy Hsu asked, sitting down next to Breezy. "Are you ready for this?"

Breezy grinned at Jimmy. He had come out of no-where a few months ago, slugging home runs all over Hampstead. Breezy hoped Jimmy wasn't just a flash in the pan because he was a really nice guy. Besides, she loved a good challenge, and it was nothing if not a challenge to pitch to a hitter like Jimmy Hsu when their two teams played each other in the regular season.

"I never knew this place was so big!" Peter exclaimed, dropping onto the grass next to his two teammates. "I feel like everything I say is going to echo."

"Yeah, I know what you mean," Breezy replied, nodding. "It is huge. Imagine playing every game here."

"I can't," Jimmy admitted.

"I *can*," Peter said, grinning confidently. "Don't worry, guys. I'll send you season passes when I hit the majors."

"Box seats, I hope," Breezy shot back, standing up. "Coach Chang's yelling for everybody. We better head in."

The three of them jogged into the dugout. Breezy sat down and took off her baseball cap. She tightened her ponytail holder and swung her legs back and forth as she listened to Coach Chang give his "get psyched" speech. It was very different from Ro's hairdressing analogies, but Coach Chang's speech was good. Still, that didn't make the team forget that Wemble had won the last 10 All-Star Games.

When Coach Chang was finished, all the players who were starting began milling around, waiting for Wemble to show up. Wemble was outside the stadium doing their warm-ups. That was a bit much, Breezy thought. It wasn't as if the element of surprise would help Wemble. If they were so good, it didn't make a difference if Emblem saw them before the game or not. Of course, Breezy thought with a grin, maybe they weren't that good. Maybe they were just playing head games.

Looking around the dugout, Breezy couldn't believe how different it was from the Emblem dugouts. Every bat had its own cubbyhole and there was even a television hanging in the corner. It was unreal.

"This is some scene, huh?" Terry asked, plopping down next to Breezy on the bench. "Totally wild."

"I know what you mean," Breezy agreed.

"Have you looked at the stands lately?" Terry asked, jerking her head toward the front of the dugout.

"They're filling up?" Breezy asked. She hadn't really been paying too much attention to things in the last 40 minutes or so. She had too much nervous energy.

"Take a look."

Breezy stood up, walked over, and peered up the dugout steps. "Yikes!" she breathed. The stands were huge, but they were almost half full. All those people were there to see them play. Unbelievable.

Sitting back down, it took Breezy a moment to realize Terry was grinning at her. "Like I said, some scene, huh?" Terry asked.

Shaking her head, Breezy tried to focus on baseball and the game that was about to begin.

"Ladies and gentlemen!" an announcer suddenly called out. "Welcome to the 20th Annual Maryland Baseball League All-Star Game!"

The crowd roared. Breezy and Terry looked at each other and giggled. Breezy was not about to tell Terry how unnerved she was that there were so many people watching. But she was glad to see that Terry seemed to be feeling equally awed.

"Please welcome the Eastern Maryland Baseball

League!" the announcer yelled.

"Let's go, people!" Coach Chang called out after the roar of the crowd faded a little. "Onto the field. Let's go!"

Breezy grabbed her hat and followed her teammates up the dugout stairs and lined up next to home plate. She looked around the field, willing herself not to stare into the stands. She could get lost out there. There was a microphone standing by the pitcher's mound.

"And our defending champions, the Western Maryland Baseball League!" the announcer added as the Wemble team trotted out from their dugout. They lined up on the other side of home plate.

"Whoa!" Breezy exclaimed softly.

"You can say that again," Peter said from next to her. "Those guys are huge! Are you sure they're in seventh grade? They don't look like it."

"What are they feeding those guys?!" Terry added. "Some of them are bigger than Hector! And he's really big!"

Breezy shot a look at Hector Martinez, who was standing at the end of their line. He was easily the biggest guy on Emblem's team. Breezy could see why he was such a good football player — he was totally solid. In fact, he probably could have played on the high school's football team. Yet some of the Wemble guys were bigger than he was. She took a deep breath.

"I wonder which one is Duane Robinson," Terry continued.

"The big dude at the very end," Peter pointed out. "That tall guy with the high-top fade. You see him?"

"Him?!" Breezy exclaimed, looking down Wemble's line. "I thought he was a coach or something."

The three of them laughed nervously.

"Please stand for our National Anthem," the announcer said.

Breezy watched a large bearded man saunter out to the microphone. He cleared his throat and started to sing. Opera singer, she thought immediately, tuning him out.

Whipping off her hat, Breezy's mind wandered during the anthem. She could easily see why Wemble had won so many All-Star Games. They looked very put-together with their matching league uniforms. Emblem players just wore their individual team uniforms. But major league players wore their individual team uniforms in the All-Star Game, so Breezy figured that Emblem was the more professional team. Wemble was just playing another head game.

Shifting uncomfortably in her pink uniform, Breezy suddenly had a flashback to Andy Gable. She shook her head, willing her mind to clear. This was not the time to dwell on that. She had to be totally focused if they were going to win this game.

After the opera singer had finished singing, Breezy followed everyone else back to the dugout. The team sat there in total silence as Coach Chang read the starting lineup.

"Top of the order — Brennan, Martinez, Chou," he said, looking at his clipboard. "Let's get off to a good start and get them off balance, okay? You can do it!"

No one said anything.

"I didn't think they'd be so big," Billy Chou finally said.

Breezy knew this was no way to talk or think if Emblem was going to have even the slightest chance of winning. "Come on, guys," she said, grinning at everyone. "If they're that big, they're probably slow, right?"

Terry smiled. "Even if they are big, it doesn't mean that they can play baseball," she added. "Maybe they recruited a football team or something, trying to psych us out."

Peter laughed, breaking some of the nervous tension in the dugout. "Well, we'll know if they start running patterns all over the outfield," he said. "Let's make an impression on them. Iceman, you lead off. Start off with a hit, okay?"

Iceman nodded his head. "That would announce our presence with authority," he replied with a cocky grin.

"Sure would," Hector agreed, handing Iceman his favorite black aluminum bat. "Get out there and announce."

"Come on, Ice!" Terry shouted as Iceman walked to the on-deck circle.

Breezy watched him take a few practice swings, psyched to see that everyone was really getting into the game now. If the Emblem team didn't think they had a chance of winning before the game started, they were already beaten. A positive attitude was so important. It was one of the very first things Breezy had learned when she started to play sports.

"Ice! Ice! Ice!" the dugout started chanting.

"Batter up!" the umpire called, and with that the game began.

Iceman walked over to the plate and glared at the pitcher, pushing his sunglasses up on his nose.

For the first time, Breezy glanced at Wemble's pitcher. She gasped. He was a monster! Checking her program, Breezy found out his name was Raymond Castaneda and he was 13 years old. He looked more like 16.

"Someone said they're going to be clocking pitches today," Breezy heard one of her teammates say as she ran her finger down the column of Raymond's stats.

"Snap!" she exclaimed, showing the book to Terry. "This guy's no football player."

Terry read the stats and grinned at Breezy. "Don't show this to anyone else, okay?"

Breezy nodded her agreement. "Let's go, Ice!" she screamed to her teammate. "Freeze him out!"

If Breezy hadn't been watching, she never would have believed it. Raymond wound up and delivered a super-sonic fastball right up the middle of the plate. Iceman didn't even twitch.

"Stee-rike one!" the umpire called out.

"Folks," the announcer began loudly, "Raymond Castaneda's first pitch, a fastball, was clocked at sixty-five miles an hour!"

Breezy groaned as she watched all her teammates in the dugout start flipping through the program searching for Raymond's stats. She guessed that she and Terry couldn't have kept Raymond's ability a secret much longer anyway. He was good and that was clear to everyone in the stadium.

Iceman got his bat around on the next pitch, but it wasn't even close to the ball.

Breezy let out a long breath. Raymond had just thrown the sneakiest slider she had ever seen outside of the majors. And the guy didn't have any attitude at all. He just wound up and delivered. No glares, no mind games, nothing like that. He just threw perfect pitches. Breezy guessed that when you were that good, you didn't need anything but your arm.

Before she could blink again, Iceman was on his way back to the dugout, his bat dragging behind him.

"Don't worry about it, Ice," Terry said, patting him on the back.

"That guy is incredible," he said, chucking his bat back into its cubbyhole. "Did you see that fastball? I sure didn't. It hit the mitt before I even caught a glimpse of it. That dude should be in the majors or something. Is he really only thirteen?"

No one answered him. Instead, Jacob Stein handed

him a program. Iceman glanced at Raymond's stats and then sighed. "Great," he finally said. "I really announced our presence out there, huh?"

"Don't worry about it," Coach Chang said, walking over, carrying his clipboard. "We're just feeling them out. Don't be hard on yourself."

"Come on, Hec!" Iceman yelled, watching the big guy step into the batter's box.

Hector took a few mighty swings and faced Raymond. Breezy grinned. The big guy looked real confident. He wasn't showing any fear. Breezy thought that was the only way to bat.

"Let's get something going!" Breezy called out, knowing that if anyone could hit off this guy, Hector could. He was ferocious.

Raymond nodded at his catcher's signal and went into his windup. His fastball caught the outside corner of the plate and Raymond caught Hector looking.

"Stee-rike one!" the umpire called.

"That's a beautiful thing," Breezy said before she could stop herself. As a pitcher, she couldn't help but admire Raymond's ability. But she knew she shouldn't let anyone else overhear her.

Four pitches later, Hector was walking down the dugout steps. "That guy is unreal!" he exclaimed. "I couldn't get anything going on him. He's like a machine."

Great, Breezy thought. That was all Billy Chou needed

to hear before he stepped up to the plate.

"Let's go, Billy!" Terry called. "Don't worry about it!" Then she turned to Breezy. "He's worried about it. I mean, I know he's a great shortstop and all, but . . . ."

"I know what you mean," Breezy agreed, nodding her head. "He *did* win a Golden Glove Award in his town last year, but he's such a timid batter."

"These guys are really good," Jacob commented. "They're going to kill us at bat. How can we stop them?"

"*Raymond* is really good," Breezy corrected, getting a little annoyed with the negative attitude in the dugout. "That doesn't mean diddly about the rest of the team."

"Breezy's right," Peter agreed. "Let's not give up."

Breezy shot him a grateful grin and turned to watch Billy strike out in four pitches. She was surprised Raymond even threw balls. Then she realized he played with the corners of the plate so much, it was a wonder he didn't throw more balls. He couldn't pitch like that and always get strikes. He just couldn't. No one could.

"Come on, guys!" Breezy encouraged as the team took the field. "Let's go, Ice!"

"You guys can do it!" Terry added.

"See you in a few," Peter said, with a cocky grin at Ice. Then he sat down on the bench next to Breezy.

Breezy smiled at him, glad that some people on the team had a positive attitude. The first inning wasn't over yet. This was baseball. Anything could happen.

11

"What's happening over there?" Breezy asked Terry. "I can't see."

"Me neither," Terry responded. "I can't take this. How do those major leaguers do it?"

It was the bottom of the third inning and Breezy was throwing warm-up pitches in the bullpen. Since this was a major league park, the relief pitchers were allowed to warm up before they got into the game. Breezy was grateful for the opportunity to loosen up her arm, but she still felt kind of out of it. It was weird not to be right there watching the action on the field.

"Let's see a fastball," Terry ordered, crouching down.

Breezy stared at the ball in her hand for a moment, and then went into her windup. She fired the ball into Terry's mitt.

Thwack! Her pitch hit her catcher's mitt — hard.

Terry laughed, pulled her hand out of her mitt, and started shaking it. "You are smokin' today, girl!" she exclaimed. "We're going to show Wemble that we've got to be taken seriously. They won't get a thing off of you."

"Let's shut them down!" Breezy agreed.

After a few more pitches, the girls heard loud cheers from the crowd. "The inning must be over," Breezy commented. "Maybe we should head back in."

"Sounds good," Terry replied. "What are we at now, the top of the order?"

"Ice struck out," Breezy said. "Whoever's Number 2 is up now."

"Do you think we'll get to bat?" Terry asked. "I would like a chance to get back any of those five runs they've got on us."

"I know what you mean," Breezy agreed emphatically as the two girls walked back to the dugout. "I wonder who's going to be pitching for Wemble now. Raymond can't stay in, right?"

"Yeah," Terry agreed.

"How are you feeling?" Coach Chang asked, as soon as Breezy and Terry got to the dugout. "Are you ready to pitch?"

Breezy shot a look at Terry and grinned. *"We're* ready," she replied.

"Great," the coach said, holding up his clipboard. "Okay, here's the new order. Hsu, DiPaolo, Stein, Morant, Hawk, DiSunno, Hayes, Tolhurst, Hooks. DiPaolo, you lead off this inning."

"Great!" Breezy exclaimed. "I can't wait to bat!"

"You're not going to get up, Breezy," Billy said.

"Everyone's struck out. One, two, three."

"Ian Delaney walked," Terry pointed out.

"Don't be so down on Emblem," Breezy said shortly.

"When you've played an inning against them, you can say whatever you want," Billy replied tiredly. "Until then, stop picking on me."

Breezy gritted her teeth and plopped down on the edge of the bench.

"I thought he could only pitch three innings!" Tony DiPaolo suddenly exclaimed. "What's he doing?"

Breezy glanced out at the field and saw Raymond Castaneda on the mound again. Then she stared at him.

"Wait a minute!" she exclaimed. "What is this guy? A switch pitcher? He pitched lefty the first three innings and now he's a righty?"

Jacob groaned. "It's his twin brother, Juan," he said, holding up the program.

"Twin brother!" four people exclaimed at once.

"I don't believe it!" Will Morant said, shaking his head.

"This is like a scene from a horror movie," Breezy agreed. "Worse than my worst nightmare."

"Maybe he's not as good as Raymond," Peter commented, trying to look on the bright side.

"Right," Hector said, sounding depressed. "Watch him warm up. I hate to say it, but he looks *better* than Raymond."

Breezy groaned. Emblem's team had not even been

able to get a piece off Raymond in the first three innings. What were they going to do now? Wemble was winning 5-0 and it wasn't looking good.

And it didn't look any better midway through the fourth inning. Emblem was out one, two, three, and the team's morale sank even lower. They took the field slowly.

Terry walked over to the mound with Breezy.

"Let's go, Parrots!" someone screamed from the stands.

"Come on, Ter! Come on, Breeze! Show 'em what you're made of!" someone else yelled.

Breezy grinned at Terry and they scanned the crowd. "There they are!" Terry exclaimed, pointing to the stands above their dugout. The entire Pink Parrots team was there with Ro, taking up a whole row. They were all wearing their uniform tops and caps.

Smiling and waving, Breezy suddenly felt like crying. She *never* cried. But she was so happy to see all her teammates right there cheering them on. She knew they weren't mad at her anymore. They couldn't be. And Breezy definitely wasn't angry with them. They had come all the way to Baltimore to watch her and Terry play.

"Go birds!" Ro called out.

Terry slapped Breezy's glove. "Come on, girl," she said, grinning and winking at her. "Let's show Wemble what these two birds can do!" Then she turned and walked toward home plate.

"This place doesn't look so big anymore!" Breezy called after her, laughing. And suddenly it didn't.

Shaking out her arm, Breezy knew she was ready. She felt loose and strong — better than she had in a long time.

"Batter up!" the umpire called out.

A big guy stepped up to the plate. Then again, Breezy thought, they were all big. Breezy was glad Terry had studied the stats of most of Wemble's players and talked to Hector. She had no idea what to throw to this guy.

Holding down three fingers and patting the outside of her leg, Terry called for an inside sidearm fastball. Breezy took a deep breath and put her feet on the rubber. Suddenly, she thought of Andy Gable. She hadn't thought of him in a few innings, and then there he was again, dropping to the dirt in her mind.

Breezy shook her head and threw the ball. It was really far outside and Terry had to scramble to get it.

"Ball!" the umpire called out.

Terry shot a concerned look at Breezy as she tossed the ball back to her.

Change-up, Breezy thought, as Terry gave her the signal. She took a long, deep breath, trying to will Andy out of her brain. Breezy glanced toward the batter. He looked as if he was standing awfully close to the plate. Why couldn't he take a step or two backward, she wondered.

Breezy delivered three more outside pitches in a row.

"Take your base!" the umpire called out, stepping forward to dust the plate off.

Shaking her head violently, Breezy began walking around the mound. "Get a grip, Breeze," she muttered. "This is the *All-Star Game*. Either you belong here or you don't. Pitch like you do."

Turning back toward the plate, Breezy was surprised to see Terry still crouching behind it. She had expected that her catcher would have come out to the mound for a little "heart-to-heart" to settle her down. But Terry was just staring at her calmly.

Breezy watched the next big Wemble batter step up to the plate and dig his back foot into the dirt. She shook out her arm and told herself over and over that he wasn't standing too close to the plate. But it didn't work. She threw four more straight outside balls.

"Take her out," someone called from the stands.

"Put in Golden, Coach," someone yelled from the outfield, referring to another pitcher on Emblem's team.

Breezy spun around angrily. Someone on her own team wanted her to be taken out? She scanned the field, but no one would look at her. Except Peter — he gave her the thumbs-up sign.

Clenching her jaw, Breezy turned back to Terry. This time the catcher had called time and was heading toward the mound. She blew a big bubble as she stopped in front of Breezy.

"What's going on, Breeze?" she asked calmly.

"Do you want me taken out, too?" Breezy questioned belligerently. "Do you?"

"Chill, girl," Terry replied, grinning. "They don't know any better. Hey, did you know that Andy Gable's up there behind home plate? Five or six rows up."

"He is?" Breezy asked, totally surprised. This was not how she had expected this little chat with Terry to go.

"Yup," Terry answered. "See him?"

Breezy scanned the stands behind the plate. Andy Gable was sitting there, bold as day, wearing sunglasses and lounging back in his seat. "He looks fine," Breezy commented, feeling a little confused.

"Sure he does," Terry said. "I even heard he's got a date with Gwen tonight."

"Gwen?" Breezy asked in shock. "Seriously?"

"Yup," Terry said again. "Really bad taste, huh?"

Breezy laughed. "I'll say."

"Listen, Breeze," Terry said after a short pause. She blew another bubble. "I think it's time to show these dweebs what you've really got for a right arm."

"You mean . . ." Breezy began and then paused, looking around. "Do you think they're ready for it?"

"Definitely," Terry replied, turning back toward home plate. She took three or four steps, stopped, and spun around. "Let 'em know you've got a rocket launcher for a right arm!"

Breezy grinned and then laughed out loud. She had to admit she loved it when Terry joked that she had a rocket launcher for an arm. Terry sometimes told her she had to soak her catching hand after a game — Breezy had thrown that hard.

"Get on with it!" a voice called from the stands.

"Get her out of there!" someone else yelled.

Suddenly, Breezy was good and mad. She was mad at the guy on her team who wanted her taken out. She was mad at the fans in the stands who wouldn't give her a chance. She was mad at the guys on Emblem who had given up already. And she was mad that she had given those guys on base free walks. It wouldn't happen again.

Jamming her hat down farther on her head, Breezy gritted her teeth and faced the plate. Terry called for an inside fastball. Time to catch these guys off balance, Breezy thought. She was about to serve them notice that Emblem had not rolled over and died.

Breezy blasted a rocket over the plate, catching the inside corner and brushing the batter back.

"Stee-rike one!" the umpire called out to the surprised batter.

"All right, Breeze!" one of the Parrots called loudly. "Show 'em what you're made of!"

Firing in another fastball, Breezy watched as the batter tried to get his bat around in time. He didn't, and her pitch thumped into Terry's mitt. The catcher grimaced, holding her hand, and then grinned at Breezy.

The batter got a piece of Breezy's next pitch — a change-up. But he swung upward and popped the ball right over his head. Breezy ran in and then stopped short as Terry jumped up, throwing off her mask.

"*You've* got it!" Breezy yelled. She saw Terry laugh just before the ball fell into her mitt.

"One away!" Peter called from the outfield. "Way to go, Breeze!"

"Nice catch, Ter!" Iceman yelled from the dugout steps. "Way to hustle!"

"Play's to first or second!" Coach Chang screamed. "Let's go, Emblem!"

Juan Castaneda stepped into the batter's box. He crouched into his stance and looked at Breezy. She couldn't believe that he looked so unflappable. He batted the way he pitched — no emotion. "Time to shake you up," Breezy muttered to herself.

Terry called for a change-up. Good move, Breezy thought. He would probably be expecting a fastball. She shook out her arm as if she needed a lot of power on this pitch. Then she went into her windup and delivered the sneakiest change-up she had ever thrown. Breezy, herself, was surprised at how slowly it approached the plate.

And Juan was caught off guard as well as off balance and he swung way too soon. He spun around as the umpire called the strike as if he didn't really believe it.

"Beauty!" Jacob called out. Suddenly, the infield was alive with chatter just the way Breezy liked it.

"Cool," Breezy muttered, looking for Terry's next signal.

Blowing a bubble, Breezy threw a sinker that dropped as if it had been shot. Juan got caught looking and some of his reserve began to crack. From her position on the pitcher's mound, Breezy could see that his teeth were clenched and his jaw was twitching.

"One more!" Coach Chang called.

"BREE-ZY! BREE-ZY! BREE-ZY!" the row of Parrots started chanting. Then more people joined in. Breezy had thought the fans were pretty loud at her last game, but this was absurd. She shot a glance at Terry, hoping her catcher wasn't getting mad. Instead, Terry was grinning and giving her the sign for a heater — her *fast*ball.

Breezy put both feet on the rubber, hands in front of her, and crouched a little from the waist. Kicking up her left leg, she pivoted on her right foot and brought her right arm back. And then she launched a rocket.

Holding her breath for an instant, Breezy waited for the crack of the bat. *Thunk!* she heard instead. Breezy exhaled as Terry held up the ball.

Breezy smiled in relief. She had found her groove and it was going to take a lot to shake her loose from it. The next Wemble batter went down swinging in four pitches.

Grinning, Breezy trotted toward the dugout. She may have walked two Wemble players but that's where they had stayed — stranded on base. Breezy knew it was the only way to come back from a start like that.

"Way to fire it!" Iceman congratulated her as she ran into the dugout and grabbed her batting helmet.

"Where's my bat?" Breezy asked in a panic. She couldn't find her wooden bat anywhere, and she was up first.

"Here you go," Hector said after a few minutes of searching. "Someone put it all the way back here."

"Snap!" Breezy exclaimed. "My poor bat. Now it's time to start something."

"There you go," Terry agreed. "Right guys?"

"We haven't been able to get a piece of either Castaneda all day, Breeze," Jacob said. "Good luck."

"Lighten up," Breezy replied, as she headed up the steps. "Don't leave me hanging. If I get on, somebody better bring me home."

"When you get on," Terry said, pulling out bats, "you can count on me."

Putting on her helmet, Breezy stepped into the on-deck circle. She dropped a weighted donut onto her bat and swung it over her head, loosening up her shoulders.

"Let's get some numbers on the board, Breeze!" Kim called from the stands.

Breezy found her friend in the crowd and nodded. Jazz and Crystal gave her a thumbs-up. Then the row of Parrots did a wave for her. Breezy cracked up. Her team was really too much.

"Batter up!" the umpire called.

Stepping up to the plate, Breezy dug in her back foot and took a few check swings. Then she faced Juan. Suddenly, he didn't seem so unflappable. Breezy stifled an impulse to grin. He looked as if the first pitch was going to be personal as he went into his windup. It was a fastball, and Breezy couldn't believe how fast it really was. It flew over the plate before she could even think about getting her bat around.

"Stee-rike one!" the umpire called out.

Breezy stepped out of the box for a moment and tapped some dirt off the bottom of her cleats. Mentally, she gave herself a little shake. She knew that it was very important that she get on base. It didn't matter how. Out of her whole team, only Terry and maybe Peter and Ice thought she could get on base. So she had to show them that she could. She had to start something. She just had to. Otherwise Emblem was looking at its 11th straight loss.

With new determination, Breezy stepped back into the box. Juan looked a little more stoic this time as he went into his windup. Breezy gritted her teeth and shifted her weight slightly as the ball came zooming toward the plate.

Her bat was a blur as she brought it around and she gripped tightly as she made contact. Unfortunately, she had swung a little late and didn't get a full swing. The ball shot into the stands behind Wemble's dugout.

Breezy took a deep breath as the catcher threw Juan a new ball. At least she had made contact, she figured. Now that she knew she could do that, she only had to straighten it out. Breezy just had to make sure to get her bat around a little sooner.

Patting the top of her helmet, Breezy faced Juan again. He tried to catch her napping with a crafty change-up, but Breezy saw it coming. Forcing herself to wait, Breezy tightened her hands as the bat began to vibrate when it hit the ball.

The ball zipped up the third baseline in a hard line drive. The third baseman didn't get a jump on it and the ball shot out to leftfield. Breezy dropped her bat and sped toward first base.

Totally focused on reaching the bag, Breezy didn't even know if the ball had been fielded. She overran the base and trotted back realizing that Juan had the ball.

Emblem's dugout exploded. "All right, Breeze!" Peter Tolhurst screamed. "Way to go!"

"Come on, Ter!" Breezy screamed to Terry, who was up next. "Let's see that hangtime you're famous for!" Terry was known for hitting these mammoth shots that appeared to hang in the air forever.

As she dug in, Terry shot a ferocious monster look at Juan. He didn't look at all perturbed. Breezy wasn't worried, though, because the look meant that Terry was going for it.

"Go, Ter!" Jazz called from the stands as the Parrots did a wave for Terry.

Juan shot a very inside fastball toward Terry, wanting to brush her back and keep her off balance. Breezy saw Terry shift her feet back as soon as she realized what was coming. Her bat was in motion a split second later. *Thwack!* The bat hit the ball solidly. Terry swung around, holding her follow-through out for a long moment as she admired her shot rising away from her in a high arc.

Breezy watched the ball go up and up and up. "It's never coming down!" she shouted gleefully as Terry's hit cleared the centerfield fence and kept going.

Jogging around the bases, Breezy pumped her fist in the air. The entire Emblem dugout emptied onto the field next to home plate. Breezy slapped hands all the way through to hit the plate. Then she turned around and saw Terry trotting in from third.

As soon as Terry hit the bag, Breezy was right there, giving her a high five. "Way to be!" Breezy exclaimed, congratulating her teammate. "You're the next Mickey Mantle!"

"You paved the way," Terry replied.

Then Iceman came out of nowhere, lifted Terry up in a massive hug, and spun her around. "You really announced our presence!" he shouted as everyone headed back to the dugout.

Spirits were now running high. Emblem had gotten some numbers on the board. The score was 5-2, so now they were only behind by 3.

Earl Hayes drew a walk and then Peter knocked him to second. Alfonse Hooks advanced them both a base with a beautiful sacrifice bunt.

One out, men on second and third, and Jimmy Hsu

was up. He proved that he was no flash in the pan when he sent a perfect line drive shot right over the right-fielder's head for a double. Earl and Peter scored and suddenly it was a one-run game.

Tony DiPaolo hit a single to leftfield. And Jacob Stein followed that up by drawing a walk. Bases loaded. Breezy was definitely beginning to see cracks in Juan's attitude. The unflappable dude was crumbling.

Will Morant struck out. Breezy hit a high pop to center. The centerfielder bobbled the catch and Jimmy scored. That made the game tied at five apiece.

The fans were going wild. Emblem was really giving Wemble a run for their money. It looked as if it was going to go down to the wire.

Then Terry struck out, ending the inning.

Breezy was picture-perfect in the bottom of the fifth. She threw seven pitches — striking out two batters and getting the third to pop up right to Billy at shortstop.

"Ladies and gentlemen," the announcer began at the end of the fifth. "It's all tied up at five as we go into the sixth and final inning. This is baseball at its best, folks."

Juan suddenly seemed to find his groove again and struck out Earl on three straight pitches to start off the sixth inning. Peter worked the count to three and two before pulling a weak hit to short center. Head down the whole way, Peter barely beat the throw to first by a nanosecond. Juan looked mad and fired three rockets at Alfonse, who didn't even twitch. Two outs.

"Come on, Jimmy!" Breezy yelled as he stepped into the batter's box. "Let's finish them off! We only need one!"

Winding up, Juan delivered a supersonic fastball. The end of Jimmy's bat caught a piece of it and sent it up and over the backstop. Juan went right into his windup as soon as his catcher tossed it back. It was clear to Breezy that pitching was all business for the Castaneda twins.

Jimmy fouled off the next three pitches in a row. Excitement in the dugout was reaching a fever pitch with two outs and two strikes in the last inning. Extra innings were not played in All-Star Games. It was now or never.

"Come on, Jimmy!"

"Blast it!"

"Send it out of here!"

"You can do it!"

Juan's next two pitches were fouled off. Jimmy was getting his bat around, but just not fast enough. Breezy thought people were going to start fainting soon, the way they were screaming and carrying on in the stands.

Juan nodded, accepting his catcher's sign. He crouched a moment and then went into his windup. Breezy caught her breath as Jimmy brought his bat around.

The crack of the bat hitting the ball reverberated through the stadium. The whole dugout fell silent as they all followed the path of Jimmy's hit. It was a low line drive hit above the third baseline. Jimmy had packed so much power on it that it didn't show any signs of slowing down. Breezy bit her lip, wishing the ball to go fair. It was too close to call.

Finally, it cleared the fence — to the right of the post! A home run! The Emblem dugout erupted, screaming and yelling. Peter scored and Jimmy trotted around the bags, grinning the whole way.

Everyone spilled out to greet him. Emblem was ahead 7-5! Finally, the team calmed down and Tony went up to bat. Juan was pretty mad and struck him out with three pitches — all clocked at over 60 miles per hour.

"Okay, team," Coach Chang said as the players headed out to the field for the second half of the last inning. "This is it! We've had a great comeback these last three innings. But we've got to hold them. Focus! Don't start celebrating yet!"

Breezy nodded as she grabbed her glove and trotted out to the field. Coach Chang was totally right. They had to hold Wemble. If they had come this far, only to lose it now . . . Breezy couldn't bear to think about it. It couldn't happen.

She took a few warm up pitches, testing her arm. It still felt pretty loose and she was getting a lot on the ball. She looked for the first batter to step up.

"Batter up!" the umpire yelled, starting the last inning.

The huge Wemble batter dug into the batter's box and glared at Breezy. She glared back. If they were going to get anything off of her, they were going to have to fight for it. The time for giveaways and walks was over.

Terry called for a sidearm fastball. Breezy almost shook her head because she thought the guy would be expecting a fastball for the first pitch. Then she realized that she had to trust Terry. The catcher really knew what she was doing. Besides, if Breezy was questioning Terry's signals, she was thinking too much. Breezy had to pitch — not think.

It was the right move. The batter was caught looking for strike one. Four more pitches and he had struck out.

Breezy tossed the ball around the infield, keeping everyone on their toes and in the game.

"Two more!" Peter called out. "We can do it!"

"The play is to first!" Breezy added. They couldn't afford any errors in this inning.

Getting the next batter to pop up to third took five pitches. But then it was two outs. And Duane Robinson stepped up to the plate.

Duane was just about everything he was rumored to be. He was huge! And he was five-for-five for the afternoon, with a single, two doubles, and two home runs. The guy was a hitting machine. If anyone could change the momentum in this game, Duane was the dude. Breezy had never seen such bat speed outside of the majors in her life.

Wondering if she had enough left on her fastball to get it by him, Breezy was a little shocked when Terry called for a change-up. If Duane knew that was coming, it would be good-bye ballpark, hello stratosphere for that ball.

Breezy decided to throw the most crafty, sneaky, mysterious change-up she had ever thrown in her entire life. Duane would be expecting a rocket, but he was going to get a slow freight train instead.

And he did. Breezy hoped that someone was videotaping this game. She had a feeling she'd want to see that pitch again and again, it was that good. Duane was caught completely flat-footed and the ball went right by for strike one.

Duane stepped out of the box as Terry tossed the ball back to Breezy. He tapped his cleats with his bat for a while and then took a few mammoth, powerful swings before moving back toward the plate.

Breezy put everything she had on her next four pitches, but Duane fouled off all of them. She had two strikes on him, but she felt as if he could keep hitting fouls all day. She didn't know if she could last.

"BREE-ZY! BREE-ZY! BREE-ZY!" the Parrots started cheering again.

"Look at that 'girl pitcher' go!" Kim shouted loudly.

Breezy grinned and shook out her arm. Kim knew exactly what she needed. She'd show Duane Robinson just what a girl pitcher could do. Nodding at Terry's signal for a fastball, she brought her arms around in front of her and stepped onto the pitching rubber. Blowing a bubble, Breezy kicked up her left leg and delivered. Even as it left her hand, Breezy knew it was scorching. The rocket launcher had delivered.

Thump! The ball hit Terry's mitt before Duane even got his bat around.

Suddenly, the whole place went quiet.

"Stee-rike three!" the umpire yelled after a moment.

Then everything erupted at once, and Breezy felt the cheers wash over her. Terry jumped up and raced out to the mound.

"You did it!" Terry exclaimed just before she engulfed her in a huge hug.

"No," Breezy protested, laughing as the rest of the team suddenly tackled both of them. "*We* did it!"